I0712472

STRANGE MEMORIES

SHORT FICTION AND POEMS FOR FLYING AND FORGETTING

ELIZABETH BEECHWOOD

Strange Memories

First edition, 2023.

ISBN: 979-8-9895100-0-9 (paperback)

ISBN: 979-8-9895100-1-6 (ebook)

Front cover image from Robert Roka

Back cover image from askhamdesign

Edited by Sarah Parke

"Yes, Yes, Yes, We Remember" originally published in Third Flatiron's *Hidden Histories* anthology (2019); "Stone Dove" originally published by Crossed Genres (2015); "Dandelion Girl" originally published in Every Day Fiction (2014); "Just Beyond the Shore" originally published in Nightscape Press's *NOX PAREIDOLIA* anthology (2019), "Dear Communist Dog Catcher" originally published in *Itty Bitty Writing Space* (2019), "Dharma Bums at Starbucks" originally published in Redwood Writers Poetry Anthology *And the Beats go On* (2014), "The Painted Ponies of Wiley Creek" originally published in Not a Pipe's *Strongly Worded Women: The Best of the Year of Publishing Women: An Anthology* (2018).

Copyright © 2023 by Elizabeth Beechwood

All rights reserved.

No part of this book may be reproduced in any form or by any electronic or mechanical means, including information storage and retrieval systems, without written permission from the author, except for the use of brief quotations in a book review.

This is a work of fiction. Similarities to real people, places, or events are entirely coincidental.

For Mom.

CONTENTS

CHAPTER I

YES, YES, YES, WE REMEMBER

On the first day of May, the Western Slope always leans in and says, "Remember that spring when the soldiers came?" As if we could ever forget. But it has become our custom to wait for her to remind us and then we bow our heads and say, "Yes, yes, yes, we remember." The Northern Peak takes up the story and says, "Remember that winter, after that spring?" And we all say, "Yes, yes, yes, we remember." As if we could ever forget.

On the first day of May, the good people of Holubica always hauled the statue of their virgin goddess out of the church and into the field. They festooned her with flowers and sang and danced in gratitude for her protection through the previous long winter. The women scrubbed themselves clean in the baths, baked nut bread, and wore their best aprons elaborately embroidered with red symbols of faith and protection. It was not a large celebration and most of the men never bothered to come in from tilling the freshly thawed soil to participate. No, it was the women who kept the spiritual aspect of the community alive.

"That May, the soldiers came from the east," the Eastern Grand Summit continues. Soldiers dressed in brown uniforms marched through our valleys and fought with our soldiers dressed in blue. They won the battle and flew their red flag in the Centrum as a sign of their power. Our people largely ignored these new soldiers. The village borders were as fluid as the Kamenec River and our people knew that the flag flying in the Centrum was not the truth of who they were, the truth that ran in their blood. They were the children of the Vysoké Tatry as much as the gentle deer and the wild Rusalka.

The brown-uniformed soldiers stayed back, out of the way, and didn't interfere with the daily lives of the people. At first, the people didn't see any difference in the new government. "Then autumn came and it was harvest time," the Southern Basin reminds us.

Yes, yes, yes, we remember.

The farmers brought in their harvests of wheat, rye, potatoes, and apples. The shepherds ushered their sheep in from the summer pastures. Men and boys chopped wood to keep everyone warm during the coming winter months. And the brown-uniformed soldiers built check-points on all the roads in and out of Holubica. Our people began to grumble. Harvests were confiscated and shipped to the new capital. Our people began to shout. Sheep were herded away. Chickens, pigs, and cows were taken. Wood was gathered to supply the insatiable needs of the soldiers. Our people took up arms. The new government clamped its iron fist upon them.

When the snow began to stick to the ground, the soldiers pulled out of the village, burning stores and warehouses as they went. They chopped the largest trees down across the road so no one could follow or return to Holubica. The village was blocked from the world, left to collapse upon itself under the heavy snows piling up in drifts. It grew quiet in the village;

no chickens fussing with each other, no cows chewing their cuds, no oxen lounging in the barns after a satisfying harvest. The market in the Centrum, usually bustling and colorful even in the winter, sat barren. People spoke in hushed voices and huddled under blankets. They rarely came out of their homes except to dash to a neighbor's house. The cries of babies echoed through our valleys and struck deep into our granite hearts.

"It did not take long for our people to begin to starve," the Southern Basin always says next.

Yes, yes, yes, we remember.

Our people began to fight with each other. They began to blame, to kill. Some hid in bunkers and caves. Some hid in basements or barns. Some congregated in the church, pleading for their virgin goddess to help them. But she was a demur goddess with a bowed head and little power.

Terecia, the deposed mayor's wife, gathered up a few of the women, women who understood, and they went to the churchyard garden. Under the grand oak was a statue of another goddess with stars on her veil and hope in her smile. Her face was upturned and her arms outstretched and the power of the Vysoké Tatry flowed up through her and into the world. The women knelt on the hard ground and burnt white candles and pleaded for the goddess's assistance.

And we heard them.

We are, after all, a manifestation of the goddess.

"We should help them," we whispered in unison to all the creatures in our valleys, on our slopes and peaks. "We must all support each other as children of the goddess."

Bear argued, "Look what they do to me! They kill my cubs in the den, they hunt me down even when I hide deep in the forest. Why should I help them? It is best if they all die."

The little Domovoi shivered in their cold hearths. "Without

the people of our houses, we have no food but, worse yet, we have no purpose to our existence. We must save the people or we will grow thin and blow away in the wind, forgotten."

Fox said, "They shoot my kind for sport and don't even eat the meat! They chop trees without regard to the life they take. And, look! They dig into the heart of you four and mine your insides and leave a mess that kills us. They throw their waste in the rivers and expect it to wash away. Why would we help them? Let them die—we will be better off without them."

We conferred and considered their words. We fussed and debated. But, in the deep bedrock of our collective heart, we knew we couldn't turn away from the people we loved so dearly. Yes, they dug into our bodies and left only death. Yes, they chopped down our trees without regard to how it affected the other trees. Yes, the people did all of these selfish things. But even as we listed the things they had done to us, we still couldn't let them die. For we had seen their love for us as well, in their festivals and in the carvings they made in their houses, in the way they cared for orphaned animals and the way they cared for each other.

We tried to keep the wind and snow from falling on the town. But it was cold, so cold and there was nothing we could do about that. The Domovoi dug into their stores of food and left as much as they could at the hearths where they had been fed for generations. The doves for which the village was named joined in since they had nothing but good from the people. They flew tirelessly into the forest to gather twigs and small branches to burn. The chickadees and nuthatches dug out seeds they had cached under tree bark and shared it with the women who came to pray to their wild goddess.

And yet, it was not enough.

Deer gave themselves up for food.

And yet, it was not enough.

The people tore down houses and burned them for heat.

The people drank melted snow with pine needles in it.

And yet, it was not enough.

The Northern Peak whispers, "And then the Rusalka came" and we huddle closer together so the Rusalka, the wild and dangerous spirits, won't hear us.

Yes, yes, yes, we remember.

The Rusalka, lured by death and easy prey, were lounging in the Kamenec River behind the church and heard Terecia praying to the goddess. "Terecia, Terecia," they sing-sanged. "Come to the river!"

Terecia knew they were the Rusalka but went to the river anyway. Her shoes crunched on the ice collecting along the shore. "What do you want from me?" she asked them in a voice that shook.

The first Rusalka laughed and tossed her wet hair over her shoulder. "What are you praying to the goddess for? Do you think she will really help you?"

Terecia was a smart woman—suspicious and smart. "I think she can—and has sent you to save us."

"Save you?" the second Rusalka laughed as a necklace of vertebrae clattered around her neck. "We have plenty to eat this winter. Why would we want that to end?"

"We'll grow fat," the third giggled as she picked her teeth with a shard of bone.

Terecia said, "You cannot grow fat on skin and bones, and that is all that is left of us."

The first Rusalka swam closer to the shore. "Even if we wanted to help you, there is nothing we can do."

"Did the soldiers block the river? Can you still swim to the other villages, the cities in the foothills? Can you bring food back to us?"

The second Rusalka laughed again, a high-pitched laugh

that was almost a hysterical scream. Terecia's skin crawled and we whispered to her, "RUN!" but she held her ground. "Why would we keep you alive? There are other people to lure into our rivers and drown."

The third stopped giggling. She whispered to her sister, the first Rusalka, "Without the people to believe in us, we will fade and blow away. And the women here are the most devout to our goddess."

The first Rusalka nodded. "We will help you."

The second Rusalka said, "What? We are the Rusalka. We do NOT help people—there are plenty of other humans to prey upon."

"Shut up," the first Rusalka said to her sister. Then to Terecia, "Of course, there is always a price."

"Of course," Terecia said. "What is yours?"

The first Rusalka tilted her head, considering, then merely smiled and dove under the cold Kamenec ice and disappeared. The other two Rusalka gave Terecia one last look, then joined their sister. Terecia shivered and wondered what she had just bargained away.

Food began to appear along the frozen riverbank. And warm clothing.

It was not enough to save all of the people but it did save some.

Finally, spring came as she always does. And the soldiers with blue uniforms returned and flew their flag in the Centrum. Our people came from their homes, their bunkers and barns, their caves and cabins. No one mentioned that the food had been taken and the people of Holubica had been left to die, to be exterminated not by soldiers but by each other. Our people were too tired to do anything more than take the food and clothes and seeds the new soldiers brought and return to their fields. No one could look their neighbor in the eye for years.

The purple crocuses bloomed that year just like they always did and Terecia gathered a handful on her way to the Kamenec River. The Rusalka were combing their hair along the bank where grass was beginning to grow. "I'm here to make good on our deal," she said.

The second Rusalka laughed and nudged the third Rusalka. "I always love this part," she said.

The first Rusalka swam over to Terecia and crossed her arms over her chest. "Everyone pays a price. Are you ready?"

"I am. What do you want?"

The first Rusalka looked at Terecia standing bravely on the shore, her clavicle poking out at sharp angles under her thread-bare shirt. Her skirt was ripped around its hem. The soles of her shoes were held on with leather strips. What could the Rusalka demand that had not already been taken from this woman?

"The flowers," the first Rusalka said. "I want the flowers."

Her sisters gasped. "But I want HER," the second Rusalka whined.

"What do we want flowers for?" the third Rusalka grumbled.

Terecia picked her way carefully to the water's edge and reached down to the first Rusalka to hand over the purple crocuses. And the Rusalka rose up in the water, her face upturned and her arms outstretched and the power of the Vysoké Tatry flowed up through her as she took the gift that Terecia offered, the gift of flowers.

On the first day of May, the Western Slope likes to remind us of how, after that winter, the celebration changed.

Yes, yes, yes, we remember.

The statue of their virgin goddess is hauled out of the

church and into the field where they festoon her with flowers. But no one dances or sings. Our people are quiet now, the horrors of that winter buried deep inside of them, weighing them down and choking their words, passing on to their children and their children's children, buried so deeply that we fear their hearts will crack like granite boulders. No, they do not dance or sing. Instead, the women scrub themselves clean in the baths, bake nut bread, and wear their best aprons elaborately embroidered with red symbols of faith and protection. Small sculptures of birds and deer are placed around the statues. Extra food is left by the hearth for the Domovoi that night. Flowers are thrown into the river for the Rusalka. It is not a large celebration and most of the men never bother to come in from tilling the freshly thawed fields to participate. No, it is the women who keep the spiritual aspect of the community alive.

And the women whisper, "Yes, yes, yes, we remember."

CHAPTER 2
DARK WITH THE FALL

She stepped off the asphalt in bare feet.
The air brittle with autumn,
filled with the falling asleep of birch,
the hardening of ground,
and whispering of varied thrush.
Golden aspen confettileaves sprinkled down, decorating
the frosted dirt.
The last blades of grass reached up and pulled the
sneakers off her feet.
She followed the deermoosewolf path with her
clothes trailing behind her.
Left sock. Right sock. Jeans. T-shirt. Bra dangling
from a spruce limb. Red panties poised
by the side of the pond, dark with the fall.
Leaves danced on the ripples as
she waded into the water.
The moment was so coldcrispsharp that
everything leapt into focus.
Every vein in every leaf.

Each twig against the grey sky.
Every facet of each glittering frost crystal,
stood out naked, glaringly obvious for a fraction of time.
And in that second,
that instance,
that eon,
she was immersed.

CHAPTER 3
STONE DOVE

The village of Holubica sat in a wide valley carved out by the Kamenec River, strategically placed for travel, trade, politics, and war. It had existed for so long that the villagers no longer remembered how it got its name; some said it was for the hundreds of grey doves that flew down from the mountains every winter, some said it was for the too-many stone doves carved on the headstones of their children. Our memories went back much further, however, back to the murmur of ocean tides and shifting tectonic plates. We remembered the first travelers who called our valley home, and why the town was named for doves.

We were surprised when people created trade routes over our slopes and through our valleys; their curiosity and industry intrigued us. We broadened our shoulders as best we could to accommodate their wagons, and shook clouds from our heads so their gardens could flourish. More people came. Many stayed.

It was the autumnal equinox when the soldiers converged on our valley from all compass points. They torched the few wooden buildings, overtook the homes, and conscripted most of the men and boys. Many women, children, and elders escaped into our forests and hid in our caves. We gladly sheltered them, turning our backs against the bullets and violence. From our caves, the people watched the plumes of war rise up. The women and children cried for their fathers, their friends, their lovers. We cried with them, large drops of slushy snow that prevented the soldiers from climbing our slopes.

Two months after the initial attack, Danica's time came with no midwife in the camp. It was the women's custom back then to return to their mother's home, or to travel to the nearby village of Zborov, to deliver their children, but Danica had been caught up by the war before she could leave. She labored far longer than the other women thought necessary, but they did not know what to do. Danica, exhausted and certain that she and the baby would die, cried out to her virgin goddess for help.

We were touched with a deep sadness for this woman. We were tired of blood and muskets and death. These were our people. Surely we could aid in some manner? We bowed our heads together and conferred.

We heaved up a rock, grey and speckled, from our western slope. It tumbled, bounced, fell from a cliff and, half-way down, it transformed. It unfurled wings, a head, and a tail, and flew to the entrance of the cave where the woman, Danica, labored. When its feet touched the ground, our dove transformed again, into a young woman. Her eyes remained the color of granite and our mud matted her long silver hair.

Danica's prayers turned to screams as another contraction struck and that was when our dove appeared in her doorway. Everyone stared at the stranger until the next contraction drew their attention back to Danica. Our dove laid her hands on the woman's belly, pushed and poked. She formed words with difficulty, saying, "The baby, she is wrong."

Danica raised herself up on one elbow. "You must save her. The Virgin sent you to save her."

We did not refute the woman's statement; we had many names.

Zlata, a traveling merchant's level-headed wife, stepped forward. "What is wrong with the baby?"

"No, no, not wrong—I mistake make! She is—" our dove pointed to her feet. "She is not being head down. Her feet come first."

A wave of relief filled the room as the women understood the trouble. Then another wave, one of fear, followed. They all knew what needed to be done to shift the child.

Zlata hissed at Rézi, the goatherd. "You birth the goats, you must know how to fix this."

Rézi shook her head and stepped away. "No, my husband took care of them. I do not know how to turn the child."

The other women, huddled in the corner like hens, shook their heads, too.

Then one wrinkled foot appeared as another contraction pushed at the child.

Only one.

Zlata whispered, "The other leg must be curled up, stuck inside."

None of the women spoke and the only sound was Danica's weak gasps and cries. No one stepped forward, willing to reach into Danica's womb to shift the child.

We knew another way, however.

The sibilant sound of the wind through leafy lindens began to fill the birthing room. It turned to a soft cooing, soothing as a lullaby. The voice grew stronger in a language none of the women understood. It was our dove, kneeling at the foot of the bed, singing softly in our language, the language of water and rock and leaves and loam. Danica's body relaxed and the tiny leg drew back up.

The women stared for a moment, then Rézi grabbed our dove's shoulder and pulled her away. "She's chanting in a heathen tongue. She is calling for Satan to come and take both of their souls!"

"No, no! I am singing her into these mountains," our dove said, fighting Rézi's hold. "I am singing for her to come, that we are waiting for her here, we welcome her."

"Let her sing," Danica whimpered as a contraction eased. "Let her sing."

Our dove tore herself away from the others, and began to sing again. The other women grumbled that they would not be a part of this and left the room. Zlata remained.

The child rolled, stirred, rolled again like a rock inside of its mother, and another contraction took hold. The child felt our love, heard our words of welcome, and answered in her own way. Danica's body swelled, hardened, pushed on its own accord, but the singing calmed Danica's mind, and her labor turned productive.

After three contractions, Zlata wiped Danica's brow and said, "I can see the child's head. She has dark hair like her mother."

After five contractions, our dove cradled the child, Angelica, cooing in our own language, "Welcome, sweet child. Welcome to the Tatra Mountains."

After Angelica's safe passage into the world, our dove was free to return to us. But our love for the people had been transmitted to her heart, and she chose to remain. She showed the people where an underground stream flowed all winter, led them to a stand of fallen alder dry enough to burn, directed them to partridges and hares willing to give their lives so our people would live.

In the spring, the wild crocus bloomed and the war officially ended. A new flag flew in the marketplace. The people crawled from their hiding places and rebuilt their homes. We were not surprised when our dove joined them. Because she had no name, the people called her Mária, after their virgin goddess. It was as good a name as any other they could have chosen.

Mária took up a simple cabin along the perimeter of the village that had belonged to Janos Zajacz, a bachelor, killed in the first week of the invasion. No one complained since we hovered over the yard, casting our shadow over the rocky ground. We were happy, however, to have our dove close.

Some of the soldiers and army followers decided that this valley, this spot beside the Kamenec River, was where they would stay and grow old, feeling fortunate to have survived the war. The people who had survived in our mountains also felt fortunate to have be alive. But they also wanted to forget. It was difficult for them, however, with Mária reminding them of their dark time of hiding. When she walked confidently though what was now becoming a village, her long silver braid swished back and forth, reminding them of the silver icicles hanging from the boughs of hemlocks. As she shopped in the new Centrum, they remembered her uncanny knowledge of the forest and animals. And, after the small church was built from our granite and a priest installed, the women whispered about their midwife's incomprehensible singing that eased a woman's labor pains. They remembered that they would have died without her. But now they wanted to forget.

But Mária's song—our song—continued to calm mothers-to-be and urged reluctant babies from their wombs. Soon, there were many children running through the streets and healthy mothers in the market, thanks to the skill of our dove. She—we—loved the people and hoped that one day the people would accept her. And some did.

But most did not.

We were afraid that our dove would be lonely and so we sent doves to her, hundreds of them, each winter to keep her company during the cold harsh days.

It only caused the others to whisper behind their hands, to whisper about doves and singing and Satan.

But, still, the women called out for Mária at their most vulnerable moments. They knew our dove would come and sing their children safely into the world. And our dove went time and time again, no matter how the women whispered.

Years later, Mária's time approached. In the Centrum, Rézi, the goatherd, whispered to Zlata, the mayor's wife, that our dove was too old, too unmarried, too closed-lipped about the identity of the father, to bear a child. We whispered through our valleys that nothing wrong had been done—why would the goddess give people such capacity for love and pleasure if she expected these gifts to be denied? Rumors swirled on the wind that Mária carried the child of Satan. We knew she carried a child of the mountains. We shivered with excitement for the new life blossoming inside of our dove.

Our dove's labor was long and difficult. Danica tried to sing the child into the world, but could not get the words quite right. Zlata wiped Mária's forehead and tried to sing, too. Rézi grumbled that this was Mária's punishment and left the room. Mária tried to sing, but her contractions stole away her breath. Our babies rolled and clanked together inside of their mother. Mária's body swelled, hardened, pushed on its own accord until the twins tumbled from their mother's body, their silent grey bodies curled like stones.

Mária held our dead babies and told Zlata, "They must be returned to the mountains."

And so Mária, our dove, began to sing again. Quietly at first like the sibilant sound of the wind through leafy lindens, in a crackling voice more like a raven than a dove.

Danica, who had heard Mária's song more than any other woman, said, "Those are not the same words you use to sing children into the world."

"I am singing them back to the mountains," Mária said. "I must sing them away."

Zlata demanded that the bodies of our innocent children be buried in the church cemetery.

The priest refused to bury the bastard in consecrated ground.

The woman who polished the altar and trimmed the candle wicks (and had three healthy children, thanks to our dove) did not come, claiming illness. The housekeeper (whose grand-daughter was the light of her life) did not wash the priest's vestments or cook his meals, claiming illness. Zlata did not bring fresh flowers to the church before Mass. She made no excuse.

Two days later, Mária's children were buried in a modest grave on the edge of the cemetery, in consecrated ground among the rocks and boulders. The stonemason carved our best granite for their headstone and adorned it with twin doves. At no charge, by his pregnant wife's command.

We saw what the women did, how they helped our dove and our children. Although we wept cold tears that overflowed the Kamenec's banks, although our shoulders sagged heavily under a shawl of clouds, we felt something of our love returned to us. And that made the sorrow easier to bear.

But our Mária never attended a laboring woman again.

Instead, she sat with other children, singing a new song.

She sat with the dying children.

She sang them to us.

Others began to adorn their children's headstones with doves.

Decades passed and Mária's eyesight clouded, her fingers crooked with arthritis. She walked the cemetery, leaving flowers or brushing snow off the headstones. She did not need her eyesight to read the stones; she remembered each child, recalled each of their passings. She sang her song in a crackling voice, more like a raven than a dove.

It was Angelica, the midwife, who found Mária's body, crumpled in the melting snow beside her children's headstone. Angelica knelt beside our dove's body, and began to pray to the Virgin Mother, when the sibilant sound of the wind through the leafy lindens caught her attention. She stood and scanned the cemetery and, to her astonishment, discovered all of the children's headstones bare. She looked up to find the trees filled with grey doves, cooing to each other.

The doves sang Mária's song, and children's voices joined in, voices that grew stronger in a language Angelica did not understand, the language of water and rock and leaves and loam.

The doves took flight, their wings whistling, returning to us.

CHAPTER 4
ELDER MATER

The Elder Mater took root before Ruth's dream became a child named Amity.

At first, Amity laid in a basket and played with the patterns of sunlight the tree's leaves created. Then, Amity fed her dolls the leaves that the tree dropped. When she was older, Amity sat beneath the tree and confided her dreams.

One spring, after many springs had passed, Amity ran to the Elder Mater and whispered that she was in love. "His name is Daniel. Isn't that the strongest name you've ever heard?" The tree didn't know, but Amity's excitement was infectious and it shook with joy for her.

A month later, Amity said, "Daniel inherited a ranch in the Oregon Territory. We're getting married and moving out there! Isn't that wonderful?" The tree didn't think that was wonderful and not even Amity's happiness could stop its branches from drooping.

The morning after Amity's wedding, Ruth arrived with a shovel and bucket.

"She doesn't realize what it means—leaving everything

she's ever known and loved. She thinks life is easy." Ruth dug up an elder sproutling and carefully planted it in the bucket. "I can't stop her but at least we can send her off with a piece of home."

The tree dropped one perfect leaf at Ruth's feet.

"I'll miss her, too."

When her mother insisted that she take the sproutling, Amity laughed, calling it absurd. She had everything she needed either packed or waiting for her but she hadn't wanted to leave with an argument between them, so she tucked the bucket between the butter churn and extra wagon wheel.

At first, she and Daniel laughed at the constant wind and fierce thunderstorms of the prairie. But, as mountains rose up in their path, their optimism eroded. Measles tore through the wagon train with frightening speed. People stopped talking with each other over the campfires, afraid to get to know someone who might die tomorrow. Amity shared her ration of water with the sproutling. "We'll be in the land of plenty soon," Amity whispered. The sproutling pushed a tiny green bud out as a show of support.

The emigrants plodded along in a line across the red rocks, each wagon their own world. Items once thought necessary were jettisoned: a piano, a dresser, a crib. Daniel eyed the bucket of soil and drooping sproutling but Amity glared him into silence. "Don't worry," she cooed, "I'll carry you on my back if I have to." The sproutling stood straighter but could do little else to respond.

Somewhere east of the Boise River, Daniel was trampled by an ill-tempered horse and died in a land that didn't give a damn. Amity threw the first handful of dirt into her husband's grave with all the rage inside her, screaming that she hated him for leaving her out in the middle of this hell on earth with nothing but her broken dreams. She stormed away from the grave and curled up around the sproutling, begging it, "Please, please, don't die."

The next morning, the sproutling dropped its last leaf.

All of Amity's love could not keep it alive.

~

THE LOCALS SAID that winter was the coldest any of them could remember.

Amity didn't care; it wasn't as cold as her heart.

Tillie Williams, the owner of a hotel in Sunflower Ridge took her in and rented her a room on credit until Amity could sell the land. Amity spent most of that winter in her bed with the stick of dead elder sproutling on the floor beside her. There was nothing for her in Sunflower Ridge but she couldn't make the journey home until spring. Lying in the dark, she pretended it was summer and she was back with the Elder Mater, confiding everything that had happened, how lonely and scared she felt, how she was sure that there was nothing left in the world for her.

Spring came, as it always did, and Amity was shocked to feel the surge of hope that rose up in her like sap. She got out of bed and looked out across the grazing lands to the east. Somewhere out there was the ranch she'd inherited. She'd turned down Mrs. Williamson's offers to go out and see the land in the past, but now, somehow, the time seemed right.

~

AMITY'S RANCH house had been broken into by a large animal or human and the interior destroyed. The barn was empty. The fields lie fallow. And not even the new hopefulness in her bones could persuade her that she could make this place a home where she could raise sheep and grow crops. There was too much work for one person. The logical option was to sell and return to her mother's house. And yet ... the seed of a dream had taken root. She just wasn't sure how to nurture it.

A sweet scent caught her attention, then. A familiar scent that lured her out beyond the barn to the edge of an untilled field where a small elder tree blazed in glorious bloom.

Amity smiled for the first time in months. "You're here," was all she could say around the lump of emotion that held back more words, words of grief and hope and gratitude. She touched the smooth thin bark with her fingertips and wove a few precious flowers into her hair. Then she turned back to face the empty fields, empty barn, empty house.

In that moment, her dream sprouted up through the rich Oregon Territory soil.

Life would go on and, one day, she would place her own daughter beneath the Elder Mater to play.

"Thank you," Amity said.

The small elder tree bent one supple branch to touch Amity's face.

CHAPTER 5

THE MEMORY OF WALNUTS

I lived with my husband, Oleg, in a small blue house that had belonged to my parents until their death. My six brothers, all older and all bullies, left for America and Canada at the first opportunity. My older sister married a rich man and now lives in the city just south of my hamlet. None of them were interested in a house filled with angry ghosts. Oleg did not mind, however. Not at first. Not before we began to fill the house with the ghosts of our children.

The tree was a mere sapling then, growing in the middle of the cemetery. Its leaves sometimes settled on the headstone of my firstborn, a girl with a whorl of fine brown hair. She'd only been three days old when she died and I had insisted that a dove be carved on the top of her granite headstone. If I had known then that I would end up with a flock of stone doves, I would never have done it. Some traditions were never meant to be started.

Other traditions, like the gathering of the walnuts and the baking of nut bread, were never meant to end.

I had five doves in the cemetery and the tree was producing

a few handfuls of walnuts when a group of boys discovered the miracle. The boys knew that playing in the cemetery was forbidden, but they thought themselves brave by doing so. When they grew hungry, they thought themselves tough by smashing walnuts against headstones and gorging themselves. That night, the boys' screams echoed through the neighborhood. They reported seeing their grandparents, parents, sisters, and brothers—all long dead. They recounted their dreams and their parents recognized them as memories of the dead. Not all the boys had nightmares, however. Some reported beautiful moments with their loved ones, memories of Christmases and warm summer days, of love and laughter. When pressed on what they had done to receive these memories, the boys all confessed: they had eaten the walnuts from the tree in the cemetery.

We villagers suspected that the tree's roots embraced the simple wood coffins, taking up the memories of the dead and storing them in its fruit. The memories must have been released when the boys ate the walnuts. And, so, some of the adults went to the cemetery and ate walnuts, hoping to see the faces of their mothers and fathers, to hear the voices of their late wives and husbands. I knew I was not destined for good memories. I was afraid of what dreams would come to me from my parents or from my mother-in-law who had never let me forget that I couldn't keep my children alive. I did not eat the walnuts, but Oleg did. His screams that night were like none I'd ever heard. I tried to wake Oleg, but he was in the grips of some past atrocity that, once he woke, shaking and sweating, he refused to recount. Which was just as well; I did not want to know. Luckier women and men had the best dreams of their lives that night, however. Enough of them that a tradition took root that year.

Each autumn, the women of our hamlet went to the cemetery wearing their white aprons heavily embroidered with red thread and gathered walnuts. Each year, the tree grew taller and stronger, producing more walnuts as it approached maturity. The women, being economical with their resources and superstitious in their beliefs, only gathered enough walnuts to meet their needs. In order to feed the most people with the least amount of walnuts, it became the custom for the women to bake them into nut bread. They ground the walnuts and added honey or sugar and maybe cinnamon, raisins, or other fruit to create a delicious filling—each woman had her own recipe that she guarded like a dragon guards its gold. They mixed yeasty dough, let it rise, punched it down, rolled it out, and smeared the walnut paste over it. They rolled it up and baked it until it was a golden brown. They laughed and shared stories as they made their bread in hopes that, by invoking the memories of their loved ones who had passed on from this world, they would have dreams of that person later. There were other instructions of what a person should do to encourage the correct ancestor with the correct memories to greet you in your dreams. But, like the recipes, these instructions varied from family to family, and none were fool-proof. In death, as in life, there were no guarantees.

After Oleg was buried next to my flock of stone doves, I was left with a meager income provided by the good graces of my sister's husband, meted out grudgingly at the cost of much begging and humiliation. I often earned extra coins by taking in laundry, mending, and cleaning out chicken coops to make ends meet before having to grovel at my brother-in-law's feet again. I went from kitchen to kitchen each autumn, not for nut bread or companionship, but for warmth and plum brandy. Most often, I went to my neighbor, Agnes's, house. She had a flock of healthy children running around her yard and milk always on her table. She tried to bring me cheese and strawberries from her garden but I always turned her away. I knew it was her way of showing that she was superior to me in all things. But her house was close and her brandy was expensive, and so that fateful day found me sitting at her table.

"I'm sending a bag of walnuts to Petra in America," Agnes said as she crushed the walnuts with her rolling pin. It had been fifteen years since the tree had started to produce walnuts and there were enough nuts for everyone, so sending walnuts to her daughter would not keep others from having their share of memories.

"Will that work?" I asked. I'd known Petra since her birth and she'd always had sweet dreams of a cousin long gone.

"I sent them to her last year. Jozef Bochak was returning to the mines in Pennsylvania and delivered them to her. Petra said the memories remained but much fainter. Which is better than no memories at all. This year, since no one is going to back to the mines, I must mail them and hope for the best. We'll see how they fare."

I made note of this and a plan took root in my belly. During the Christmas celebration in the church, I approached Agnes and asked, "Did Petra receive the walnuts?"

"She did. A few were moldy and had to be thrown away, but most of them were intact," Agnes said.

"And the memories? They were intact as well?"

"Her dreams were as sweet as ever. But more importantly, she's getting married. To a man of means."

Agnes sauntered away to her warm home filled with Yuletide cheer. What did she know about suffering? Of being cold and hungry and having to beg to stay alive? But now my plan sprouted, a plan that had the winter, spring, and summer to grow fruitful. If all went well, I would have a fine harvest in the autumn.

I waited patiently, then I joined the women and gathered

an apronful of walnuts and made my own nut bread. Agnes raised her eyebrows but didn't say anything. What did she care if I suddenly decided to indulge in the memories? But instead of eating the nut bread, I rode with a farmer taking hay to the city where my sister lived. I did not go to beg from my brother-in-law, however. I stood on a corner in the Centrum and told the story of the walnuts and the memories they held. I gave away a few slices of nut bread and waited. The next day, some of the people returned, saying they'd had the best dreams of their lives. They bought up the rest of the nut bread and the walnuts I had in my pockets. Luckily for me, everything was gone before the one man came yelling and shaking his fist.

"Witch! What kind of devilish nuts are those? The nightmares they gave me were awful!"

I shrugged. "There is no guarantee whose memories you'll get. You must have terrible luck."

I walked away as he hollered at my back. What did I care? I was an old woman who would now be warm all winter long without the charity from her brother-in-law.

The following autumn, I did not bother with making nut bread. Why waste the effort and money if all the people really wanted was the nuts? I gathered the walnuts into a small sack and, although the other women glared and grumbled, I had butter and beer as well as heat that winter.

But the year after that, the merchant who lived in the grand stone mansion on the hill just below the castle came with hired men from another village. These men had axes and hammers. They stood around the walnut tree, on graves, wide-legged and menacing, challenging us with their stony faces. The women whispered, then shouted, then brandished their brooms. But they did not dare cross the men who smiled in a way that said they'd love to put those women in their places. We watched as the men gathered nearly all of the walnuts, leaving only those that were small or shriveled or not quite ripe. Looking around at the wall of angry women, hands on their hips, one had to wonder if the merchant hadn't left a few just so the women wouldn't destroy his home.

Year after year, the merchant took more and more walnuts and shipped them away. And year after year, the women were allowed fewer and fewer nuts as the merchant became greedier, until no one could make nut bread anymore.

The tradition was left to die, to wither away like a tree deprived of water.

And I was left to beg at my brother-in-law's doorstep once more.

Shortly after, Agnes went to live with Petra in America and Lucina, Agnes's granddaughter from her youngest son, moved into Agnes's house with her new husband, Hans. Hans was an outsider but, since Lucina was known to us, she was welcomed into the hamlet as if she'd lived there all her life instead of being born and raised in the city. It was a surprise when Lucina brought me a basket of strawberries from the garden behind her house.

"Are you mocking me?" I asked her. "I thought you were a good girl but here you are, pointing out that my strawberries are never as sweet as Agnes's."

Lucina just smiled and said, "I only hoped to show respect for my elder."

"Elder? Or old, useless woman?"

"You are not a useless woman. I'm sure you have many experiences that I can learn from."

She looked so sincere. She sounded sincere. I thanked her and ate every one of those berries that very afternoon. They were sweet and filled with hope.

And so it went on all summer that Lucina would bring me vegetables or eggs without seeming to expect anything in return. My small pile of firewood grew larger and larger, as if elves came in the night and added to the pile. Obviously, it was Hans, since he worked as a lumberman in the mountains, but I never saw him in my yard. I wasn't sure what to make of these two people. I stood in my kitchen one morning, drinking peppermint tea with the herbs that Lucina had grown and eating a piece of bread that Lucina had left me and watched the young couple laugh as they worked in the garden together. Agnes must have told her granddaughter about the horrible, selfish woman who lived next door. Surely Lucina knew that no one spoke to me. That she wasn't supposed to treat me kindly. That it was my fault that the merchant had learned that those walnuts were worth a lot of money.

Other young wives and daughters visited Lucina, as she was well-loved in the hamlet. It was summer still, and my windows were open and I couldn't help but overhear them as they sat in the yard and sewed as the children ran about.

"It's not right," Lucina said. "Other people experiencing the memories of strangers and treating it as a lark, a parlor trick."

"I heard that they have parties in the city," another woman said, "where they eat the nuts and then retire to rooms to sleep and dream."

"It's true," Lucina said. "I've seen it. Even having nightmares doesn't stop them. It's the not-knowing that excites them as much as the dreams do." Lucina's voice began to rise. "It's sacrilege. Taking this gift from the tree, and therefore from the Goddess herself. Have they no shame? No respect for the dead?"

I peeked out between my white lace curtains. The other women were nodding their heads and saying that Lucina was right. I was shocked to hear Lucina speaking so openly about the Goddess. Of course, we all kept small altars in the corners of our homes and many of us left food for our Domovoi, but to hear her speak so openly? I wanted to yell out to them—Take care! Don't let the priest hear you! But I remained silent in my house as another woman spoke up.

"And now the memories are exclusive to the rich. None of us can afford to even buy back any of the walnuts. We've lost our ancestors' memories."

"I'd love the chance to hear my mother's voice again," another woman said.

All around the circle, heads nodded as the young, strong women gave voice to their feelings, to their desires, to what was rightfully theirs.

I covered my ears with my hands and quickly left my house, walking as fast as I could down to the cemetery to my flock of doves where I couldn't hear any more of their wild and dangerous talk.

Come autumn, their talk and ideas turned into action. Lucina and the other young women locked arms and stood around the beloved tree and shouted at the merchant's men to stay away, that they brought disrespect to their mothers by doing this, that they were not real men at all but dogs working for cruel masters. The women were sure that their righteous anger and determination would protect them from these men. I stood across the street with a handful of older women and watched. The next morning found those young women nursing bruised faces and broken arms and doubting that their Goddess even existed anymore.

I wondered, too.

But all winter, spring, and summer, the young women continued to talk and to plan. And other women joined them. Not-so-young women. Women who owned businesses. A doctor. A teacher. A lawyer. I was shocked to see how many women came to Lucina's house. I was shocked that women could even have the type of lives these women led. And I was shocked at how small my own life had become. It felt as if it were another me who had been a young mother, a young woman with so much potential. What had happened to me? What would Oleg think of the woman I had become?

That autumn, I joined the other women at the cemetery. I had a terrible pit of dread in my stomach. Taking back the walnut tree seemed impossible. The merchant came with hired strong-men from the city who carried guns. They came with the police and the backing of the mayor, who surely benefitted from the sale of the walnuts. This time, the beatings were worse and two women even died. The women were forced back to their homes, stripped of their businesses, their professions, and many were forced to leave the hamlet that had now grown into a town.

But the worst thing that happened that year was that Lucina lost her belief in the Goddess, in the righteousness of her actions, in the power that she and the other women had to change our town.

I could not abide that.

I went to my altar in the corner of my home and lit a red candle.

"They are so brave—fighting for what I destroyed. I'm so sorry for what I've done," I whispered into the dark space around the candle. "Please help them."

There was a rumbling then. The air shook, as did the wooden floor beneath my knees. A bolt of lightning blinded me. A crack and a great thundering shook the house, toppled the red candle that caught the altar cloth ablaze. I quickly beat out the flames but my room was filled with an angry red glow. I ran to the window—the top of the walnut tree was covered in flames. Outside, I joined the others passing buckets of water down to the cemetery to try to save the walnut tree. But water could not stop the Goddess's fire. The smoke rose up from the tree in dark ghostly faces. The moans and screams of the dead filled the night sky. In the morning, the charred split body of the walnut tree smoked with the last of its life rising up into the sky.

The women gathered around the tree, tears streaming down their cheeks. No one would see the memories of their loved ones again.

Shame kept me in my house that winter. The Goddess had heard my request but she also remembered that I was to blame. She had punished me by destroying the tree. Lucina came to my door several times, calling out for me to open the door. I couldn't bear to answer her. She left me food. I couldn't bear to take it from her. I did not deserve her kindness.

One morning in the dark of winter, there was a tapping on my bedroom window. I pushed the lace curtains back and saw a dove perched on the sill of my second-floor window. It peered into my house with something round in its beak. I opened the window to a great gust of cold wind and pale feathers. The dove cooed and flew around my room, then out the window again. But not before it dropped the round object onto my small, cold bed.

There on the white bedspread was something that looked very much like a walnut.

There were no walnut trees in the area.

And yet ...

Did it contain the memories of my Oleg? My children? Would I hear their laughter again if I ate it? Could I sell it in the city? Surely it would bring a huge price that would keep me for the rest of my life.

I traced my finger along the rough, brown shell.

It was a perfect walnut. A small, perfect baby curled around itself. With nourishment and nurturing, it would unfurl. It would grow tall and straight. It would laugh in the sunshine and wave its branches in the wind.

Warmth penetrated my bones as if I'd walked out into a summer day. Tears streamed down my cheeks. I did not deserve this … and yet, there it was. Unbidden, freely given, waiting for me to accept it.

I scooped up the walnut and donned my warm coat and boots and trekked through the snow to Lucina's house, which was filled with warmth and a new beloved daughter. I stood in her kitchen and opened my fist. Lucina gasped.

"Together, we will keep it safe through the winter," I told Lucina. "We'll coax a sprout out of it in the spring and nurture the sapling along."

"And when the time is right," Lucina added, "we will plant it in the back of the cemetery and we will pray to the Goddess. With luck, no one will discover it for a long time. Not until we are strong enough to protect it."

"Yes," I said as Lucina placed her new daughter into my arms. "And when the walnuts are ripe, I will show you how to bake nut bread." I stroked the child's head where a whorl of fine brown hair curled like a walnut shell.

"I may even try a piece," I whispered to the child.

CHAPTER 6

TWO DRAGONS – RED AND GREEN

The two dragons—
they don't look the way you're expecting.
They aren't huge
with leathery wings
or scales
breathing brimstone and fire.
Instead, they are small.
Their bodies long and lithe
covered with tentacles
like a sea slug.
Their facial features show their emotions;
they do not speak.

The red dragon appears unexpectedly.
It slides out from under the paddle-shaped leaves
of the nasturtium.
You're afraid to move, to run,
or to pick up a stick and beat it back.

First it brushes up against your shins,
arching like a cat and
winding itself around your legs.
It winks at you,
or maybe that's a smirk.
You feel it's certain it has control over you.
Your breath stops as if it's already wrapped itself
around your chest.

The second dragon, the dragon you saw first,
but forgot about,
came to you in a Japanese garden
in your dream.
This dragon was a lovely woman
who did not speak.
She wore a simple dress of mottled white and green and rose
and peace was the fragrance she wore.
The woman turned to you,
on that bridge over a river,
and smiled, touched your hand, then slid into the river,
transforming into a green dragon.
She swims in the calm, slow-moving river,
her tentacles swaying with the movement of her body.
She isn't leaving you however;
she is showing you a different path.

When the memory of the green dragon reappears in your
mind,
the red dragon's grip slips.
You can wiggle a toe, then your ankle,
can shift your weight without falling.

These two dragons live
side by side.
Green and red.
Yin and yang.
Complimentary colors.
Sometimes you catch them curled up together sleeping.

CHAPTER 7

MAGICAL TRUTH

I thought there were three kinds of Truths: The Truth you can smell, the Truth you can hear, and the Truth you can see. But I was wrong.

STARA and I headed out through the sharp beach grass dunes that protected our little house from the ocean. It was Clean Up Day, which is usually my favorite day of the week because a bunch of us meet on the beach and Debbie-In-Charge hands out garbage bags and we all yell GO TEAM, except I have to bark it out. It's the only time Stara doesn't scold me for barking and all the kids think I'm funny. Sometimes I even spin around on my back legs and everyone laughs.

This Clean Up Day was different, though. The sun was out and the morning fog was disappearing over the mountains but the waves kept rumbling in and making white foam.

After we yelled GO TEAM, Stara headed down the beach

alone. We were supposed to stay together and Stara was supposed to talk to Debbie-In-Charge while I helped the kids. At first, I didn't realize she wasn't with us and then I had to chase after her with my claws digging into the wet sand and my tongue flapping. Running is glorious! The air raced over my nose but not fast enough to hide the scent. I skidded to a stop and dug out a plastic bottle that thought it could hide from me. Ha! I'm way smarter than that bottle! I trotted back to Stara with my head held high and my tail waving like a flag. That was what we did on Clean Up Day—found plastic things and put them in the garbage bag. I'm the only one who can smell the plastic hiding under the sand though. Everyone says that makes me special.

Stara took the bottle from me and shoved it into the garbage bag without saying *good girl, Scout.* She must have forgotten that she was supposed to say that when I brought her plastic. So I dug up another bottle. This time, she didn't even take it from me. I pushed it into her hand, but she was staring out at the ocean with that look that said she wasn't seeing the ocean. Sometimes Stara saw the world differently. Next, she'd take a sketchbook out of her pocket, make a few marks, and later she'd paint something wonderful from what she saw that wasn't there. What wasn't there was the Truth, she told me once. I don't understand how something you can't see can be the Truth.

Just like I'd expected, Stara reached into her pocket. Then the corners of her mouth went down and the line between her eyes got deep, which meant that something was wrong. She looked down at me and her lips turned up and I knew that should have meant that she was happy but the line between her eyes was still there. She's sad a lot lately and no matter how many kisses I give her, she doesn't stay happy. I found a dead fish on the beach the other day and brought it to her to cheer her up—rolling in dead fish always makes me happy.

Bad girl, Scout.

"I don't draw that kind of stuff anymore, remember?" she said.

Stara was an artist who worked in acrylics—she told people that all the time. When she painted, she put on happy music and danced and sang. Sometimes she pretended a paintbrush was a microphone and I'd dance on my back feet and we both laughed so hard. She was filled with joy and her paintings took their shapes from her joy.

She finally took the plastic bottle from me—*good girl, Scout*—and put it in the garbage bag and we started walking again. I tried to stay with her but I got distracted—there's always something fun to smell and see and taste at the beach. Then I caught the scent I hated most of all.

Fire.

Fire is a very bad thing that eats up everything it touches. I didn't want to find the fire, but I didn't want it to find me, either. I followed the scent to a circle of stones up near the dunes. My fur relaxed when I realized that the fire was dead and all I smelled was the burnt black wood that was left. Stara was safe from the fire! I raced down to her, my feet light again because everything was good and the fire was gone and there were seagulls standing around and I was going to run through them and make them fly and squawk and yell! I raced through the birds and past Stara, kicked up sand in a triumphant spin and raced back to her. Everything was GREAT!

Stara's hands were fists and her legs were stiff.

Was I a bad Scout?

She said *oh shit.*

Shit meant that something was very wrong. I put my nose in the wind but I didn't smell anything unusual. I listened hard but all I heard were the waves rumbling up on the beach. Then I saw them. Two kids were in the ocean, walking toward us. But not in the ocean, on the ocean. On top of the waves. The little one was a girl with dark hair and hunched shoulders. The boy was taller and held his head low. I tilted my head this way and that, trying to get a good look at them. I sniffed the air harder. The only person I smelled was Stara.

I should have smelled them. It's a Truth you cannot hide.

My fur rose up around my shoulders and I growled a warning for them to stop, to stay away from my Stara. Stara kept saying *shit shit shit.* Then she said *ghosts* like it was an amazing thing. Like it was a good thing. She pulled out her phone and took pictures and said things like *they don't show up* and *what are you?* Her voice shook. The kids opened their mouths but they had no voices.

I growled as the kids came closer. I'd never bitten a kid before, but I would to keep my Stara safe.

Then Stara did something I did not like one bit.

She led those ghost-kids over the sharp beach grass dunes to our little house.

We used to live in Portland. I stayed in our apartment while Stara went to school, but she took me everywhere else with her. Powell's. Voodoo Donuts. Saturday Market. And Lillian's art gallery. I liked Lillian. She had black hair and black clothes and dark eyes with lots of dark gray around them. At first I was afraid of all the black where it didn't belong, but her eyes smiled and she ran her hand down my neck and shoulder and didn't try to touch my face. She smelled like paint and chalk and canvas and turpentine, kinda like Stara but with an extra smell that said Lillian.

One day, Stara and I brought a bunch of paintings to Lillian's art gallery. There were big fish and orcas flying and zebras and giraffes playing on the canvases—Stara painted stuff like that, the things she saw that weren't there. It's a magical kind of Truth.

Stara told me, "I'm not even going to bother with a portfolio. She'll tell me to bring them right in for a show, anyway."

Stara propped the canvases up against a white wall and Lillian said the words *playful* and *whimsical* and *not what I'm looking for* and *grittier vision*. Stara blinked a lot. Her lips made a tight line across her face. She looked at the floor and the ceiling. She didn't look at Lillian. She said *thank you* and piled the canvases up, not even being careful of the paint. She walked out of the gallery with stiff legs.

We went to another gallery.

And another.

And another.

Back in our apartment, Stara threw the canvases on the floor. She yelled "None of them would know real art if it bit them on the ass! Whimsical is not art! This is art!" and splattered paint and went wild. I was scared and pulled the canvas with the zebras running down the beach—I liked those zebras —out of the way and hid it under the couch. I shoved my face deep under my bed so I couldn't see what she was doing. I didn't understand—she loved her paintings. They were her magical Truth.

Stara took those terrible canvases back to Lillian.

"They are grittier," Lillian said. "They'll sell. But are you sure this is the kind of work you want to produce?"

Stara growled out the words "Do you want them or not?"

Lillian put the paintings in her gallery and Stara was happy. She said things like *sold all of my paintings* and *down payment* and *I'm finally an artist.*

We moved to our little house by the ocean with one big room where I could keep watch over everything. We ate and slept and watched television on our couch. There was an awful fireplace, too, with a big, empty mouth just waiting to catch fire and eat us all up. The day we moved in, Stara hung the painting of the zebras over the fireplace and moved her painting supplies into a room called My Studio.

But, you know what? After that, she stopped carrying her notebook and pencils. White canvases sat all around her new studio. Stara stared at them. Sometimes she painted a little. But she never took any more to Lillian or any other gallery.

WHEN STARA BROUGHT those ghost-kids into our house, Girl went into My Studio right away. Stara and Boy sat on the couch looking at Stara's laptop. They pointed at things and talked to each other even though no sounds came out of Boy's mouth. Stara pulled out her cell phone. Boy pointed a lot and Stara pushed buttons but no one's voice came out of the phone. "Email?" Stara asked. Boy nodded and they went back to the laptop, pointing and pushing buttons again. It went on for a long time and I got bored. I curled up in my bed on the floor and watched Girl perched up on a shelf in My Studio, glaring at all of us.

I didn't like her one bit. There was no Truth I could figure out about her.

That night, Stara took out her charcoal pencils and sketched Boy. That really got Girl's attention and she came out of My Studio to see what was happening. She got closer. And closer. Stara was so busy sketching that she didn't notice. I growled a warning. Girl smiled at me with her little teeth showing. She touched Stara's hand and goosebumps came up on Stara's arm. Then Girl went INTO Stara. Stara's eyes looked like they saw something far away and her smell changed—she didn't smell like my Stara anymore.

She smelled like ... a different kind of Truth.

A Truth that made my ears lay flat and my lips curl away from my teeth.

If she didn't smell like my Stara, was she still my Stara? Or was she Girl? Or was she someone else, someone I didn't know or love?

StaraGirl walked into the studio and picked up a paintbrush and slapped paint onto one of the white canvases. I paced and growled—this was wrong! I looked over at Boy—he looked afraid of what was happening, too. StaraGirl just kept painting one canvas after another until Girl finally came out of Stara and went back to her place on the shelf. Stara was on the floor with her eyes closed but she wasn't sleeping and couldn't protect herself from this girl! I ran into My Studio even though I wasn't allowed to and stood over my Stara, showing my teeth to Girl just in case she thought she'd go inside of my Stara again. She stuck her tongue out at me and crossed her arms in front of her chest. She wasn't going anywhere, her body told me.

Stara groaned and sat up, holding her head with her hands. I was so relieved that a whine slipped out of my mouth as I licked her face to apologize for not protecting her like I was supposed to. She smelled like my Stara again, which was a relief because I had thought that smelling and hearing and seeing were all the Truth and since the ghost-kids had shown up, I knew that I'd been wrong and I now I didn't know what the Truth was anymore.

"What happened?" Stara asked me. I barked to tell her but she held her head tighter and said *be quiet, Scout* and then *oh shit.* My fur ruffled and I searched the room, trying to see what was shit.

Stara stared at the canvases that StaraGirl had painted. One had trees and cars and tumbling houses and screaming mouths full of teeth. One was a box full of people legs and arms and hands and heads. Another one was my Stara, but not my Stara, with a big grey blob of paint in the middle of her chest. There were two black Xs where the eyes should have been. Stara laughed—but it wasn't a laugh, it was a warning bark.

"I'm back, baby."

THE DOORBELL RANG!

The doorbell never rang!

No one ever came to the door on that side of the house!

The doorbell rang!

Stara said *quiet, Scout* and opened the door that no one ever used. It was Lillian. I didn't recognize her face at first because her lips and eyes and clothes weren't black. But her smell was still paint and turpentine and the smell that said Lillian, so I knew the Truth of who she was.

Lillian came into the house and gave me a good scratching down my back, the kind that made my eyes close and my foot kick at the air. Lillian looked around the room but didn't say hello to Boy who was slouched down on the couch. She must not have been able to see him—like I couldn't smell him. Lillian saw the canvas with the zebras, the one I'd saved, over the fireplace.

"I'm glad you kept that one," she said. "It's my favorite."

Stara's body got stiff. "The paintings are in here," she said, leading Lillian into My Studio.

Girl glared from her shelf. Lillian didn't see her, either. She stood in front of the easel and looked at the canvases that StaraGirl had painted. Stara bit her fingernails and shifted from one foot to another.

Lillian said things like *childlike enthusiasm* and *excellent distortion of perspective* and *bold choice of subject*. She rested her chin in her hand for several more tense minutes. " Scarlet Onia was scheduled for this month's Last Thursday Spotlight at my gallery, but she had to postpone. Do you want her spot?"

"Yes," Stara said without breathing.

"Can you have five more in a week? That's a lot of work."

Stara smiled and her whole face looked happy. "Yeah, sure. Do you think they'll sell?"

"If they're all this good, yes."

Lillian looked at her phone. "I have to go—I have an appointment in half an hour with a realtor. Call me on Monday and we'll talk details."

Lillian let herself out the door that no one ever used.

Stara smiled at Girl. Girl frowned at Stara.

"Cheer up!" Stara said to her. "She loved our work."

Girl stared at Stara, challenging her with direct eye contact. And Stara did not back down.

Stara shouted, "I got a reply!"

Boy's face got bright and he smiled so big that I knew for sure he was happy. I liked this kid, even if he didn't smell. Stara said things like *tell my boy he is free to go* and *do you know how to go?* Boy shook his head. They emailed his family for a while. Stara said things like *burn a photo of you* and *how about the drawing* and *that's the plan.*

I snapped to alert when Stara got the lighter out of the kitchen drawer—I knew what that lighter did.

Fire.

I barked once to warn her, to remind her about fire.

Stara didn't answer me, she didn't even say *quiet, Scout*. She took Boy's charcoal picture outside. We followed her—Boy walked through the wall and I used my doggy-door. Girl followed through the wall and sat on the porch step.

"Ready?" Stara asked Boy.

He nodded. His face was full of curves that said he was very happy.

Stara flicked the lighter. The flame burst to life. I crouched close to the ground, afraid of the fire, afraid to leave my Stara alone with the fire. Stara touched the flame to the paper and the fire jumped and gobbled it up. Boy got thinner and thinner, until I couldn't see him anymore. Stara gasped and dropped the last corner of the picture onto the concrete patio. The fire ate it up and disappeared. Stara put her fingers in her mouth— the fire had gotten her while we'd been watching Boy go. If I was a person, I would have hugged her and cried. All I could do was whine and paw at Stara's leg. I was so sorry that I'd forgotten to protect her.

"I'm okay," Stara said. She crouched and touched the pile of ash that used to be Boy's picture. "He's gone. At peace."

We turned to go back into the house. Girl stood in our way. She pointed at the spot where Boy's portrait had burned.

"Not yet," Stara told her. "We need to paint some more first."

Girl frowned and her eyes said that she wanted to do something bad to my Stara.

I growled but Stara didn't pay attention to my warning.

～

I DIDN'T ALWAYS LIVE with Stara. I'd lived with another family but they said I was too much for them. *Bad girl, Scout.* So they took me to the animal shelter where I sat waiting and waiting for that right person. A man walked by, then came back. He talked to me and tossed me some treats, but I stayed in the back of my kennel. I didn't like the way he stood with his hands in hard fists. His eye contact said don't challenge me. His smell said stay away.

But then I smelled something else, something that came and went so fast that I wasn't sure if I'd smelled it at all. I sniffed the air carefully and there it was—the smell that said Stara. I didn't know it meant Stara then, but I smelled the Truth of her. She stood back away from the kennels. Her arms were crossed in front of her chest and she didn't make eye contact with anyone. The guy said "What about this one?" He pointed at me. I looked at Stara. She looked at me. I wagged my tail and smiled at her the best I could.

"What are you going to do with a dog?" she asked the guy whose name turned out to be Nick.

"Home protection."

Nick decided I was the dog for him; I was The One.

Of course, I wasn't his The One, but I went home with him and Stara anyway.

We lived in a tall house with trees by the sidewalk. Nick let me out the back door to do my business. It was Stara who took me for walks every morning and every night. It was Stara who fed me and played with me. I slept on the floor by Stara's side of the bed and did a happy dance when she came home every day. Nick didn't like me much after the first few days. He said I didn't bark or growl enough. Stara said *good girl, Scout.*

This was all before Stara started painting and she worked in a place called a coffee shop, where dogs were not allowed. One night, Nick and Stara got in a big fight. They growled and barked at each other all the time, but that night was the worst. I hid under the bed. Then Stara's voice changed—she sounded afraid. I ran out of the bedroom. Stara was in the living room. Nick was there, too. His voice shook the walls. He grabbed Stara's arm.

I saw her skin turning red.

I RAN.

I ran at Nick and bit his pant leg and growled and pulled. I couldn't let him hurt my Stara. Nick let Stara go and kicked me, hard, in my ribs. I yelped and fell.

Stara got real mad then. She yelled at Nick and threw the remote at him.

Nick left the house and the whole house shuddered when he slammed the door.

Stara hugged me so hard that my sore ribs hurt even more but I licked her face and wagged my tail so she would know how much I loved her. Stara threw a bunch of our stuff in the car and I settled into the seat next to her. I never saw Nick again.

WE MET up with Debbie-In-Charge and her kids at the coffee shop in town.

"The Seaport Aquarium is accepting applications from artists to paint a mural on the side of their building. Your work is so cute, you should apply," Debbie-In-Charge told Stara as I waited patiently for one of her kids to drop their cake pop.

Stara's jaws clenched shut and she looked like she had something bad in her mouth. She growled "I'm too busy getting ready for a show to worry about a mural."

Debbie-In-Charge said, "Why don't you print cards and t-shirts and tote bags from your paintings? They're adorable. I'm sure they would sell."

"I want my work in the big galleries," Stara said.

"You can't do both?"

"I need to concentrate on the gallery work."

Stara said the last words in a tone that said she wouldn't talk about it anymore.

Back at our house by the beach, Stara paced around the house.

She stood in front of a white canvas in My Studio.

She opened tubes of paint. She closed tubes of paint.

When it was dark outside, Stara took a bottle out of the refrigerator, a bottle that popped when she opened it. She got that terrible, dangerous lighter out of the kitchen drawer and lit candles and placed them around My Studio. My body flinched every time a flame jumped out of the lighter

"Come on, let's get this party started," Stara said. Her voice sounded funny. "You know I can't do it without you."

I stalked closer to my Stara. I had to protect her. But, when Girl made her move, I jumped right through her. I couldn't stop her from going into my Stara.

My Stara turned into StaraGirl.

My tail stuck between my legs, tight against my tummy. I watched StaraGirl go wild, painting and dancing around the candles. She stopped and looked at the new creation.

It was a painting of Girl smiling in a white dress.

StaraGirl started to laugh. A horrible, screaming laugh that made my fur stand up all over my body. I wanted to run far away from her.

But I couldn't run. My Stara was still there. Wasn't she?

I laid flat on the floor and crept closer and closer, my paws just inside My Studio where I was not allowed to go.

StaraGirl snatched up two candles, spun around, and put

them on the easel ledge. The flame reached out and licked the canvas. Then the fire jumped out of the candle and climbed up the canvas.

The fire burned it, like it had burned Boy's picture.

The smoke got thick and black and filled the room and Girl came out of my Stara and stood in front of the painting, watching it burn.

She got thinner and thinner and then she disappeared.

I was relieved that she was gone.

But the fire didn't go. It ran across the floor and up the curtains and across the ceiling. I grabbed my Stara's arm—I couldn't bite Stara! I had to bite Stara to get her out! I pulled and pulled. I pulled Stara out of My Studio.

The fire followed us. It ate our couch.

I pulled and pulled.

It ate my bed.

I pulled and pulled.

It ate the zebras running on the beach.

I got my Stara to my doggy-door. I pulled her arm through.

But the rest of my Stara was too big.

Something crashed in My Studio.

I had to get away from the fire—I had to run!

I had to protect my Stara!

The scream that said RUN got so loud that I couldn't not listen to it.

I RAN.

AFTER THE FIRE, I lived with Lillian in an apartment above the store she bought in our beach town. The store was a fun place with lots of colorful kites and pinwheels and t-shirts and I got to greet everyone who came in. I couldn't be completely happy without Stara, though.

Stara stayed in the hospital in Portland for a while but Lillian brought me there—*Quick while no one's looking, Scout!* Stara looked a little different and smelled a little different but I smelled the Truth of her and I had to work hard not to run up and down the hospital hallway with joy. *Good girl, Scout.*

It had been the hardest thing I'd ever done—leave Stara alone with that terrible fire—but I had to do it. I had to RUN for Debbie-in-Charge who pulled Stara out through the big door.

When Stara came out of the hospital, we moved into a small house above Debbie-in-Charge's garage. Everyone came when we moved in and said things like *you look great, Stara* and *glad you're back.* Stara cried when she saw a bunch of white canvases and paints in the house and said things like *thank you so much* and *can't wait to get started.* She painted wondrous, amazing animals and the beach again. She sang into her paintbrushes and I danced on my back legs with her. She painted her Magical Truth.

We go to the beach on Clean Up Day again—I have to go since I'm the only one who can smell the plastic under the dirt —and we use trash bags that have a giant octopus on it gathering plastic with all eight of its legs. Stara drew that octopus one morning after we'd been at the beach and she saw things that weren't there and then made some marks in the notebook that Lillian gave to her.

Stara brought her new paintings to Lillian who said things like *screams summer vacation* and *be smart about your marketing* and *bring me everything.* Now, Stara's work is on t-shirts and cards and tote bags. She sells them in Lillian's store and packs her work up in boxes and mails them to people far away who order online.

Maybe terrible things have to happen to make you do what your Magical Truth tells you to do.

Every time we go to the beach, though, I watch out for more ghost-kids. I'm not sure what I would do if I saw one, but I know I wouldn't let them near my Stara.

That's my Magical Truth.

CHAPTER 8

DANDELION GIRL

Sharon Abbot lived in a house overlooking the bay—she enjoyed the view but hated the ocean. Her husband, Tom, was a commercial fisherman who went out on the ocean almost every day. Sharon had been on his ship, the *Jolly Roger II*, once in the ten years they'd been together. She hadn't lasted two hours onboard before making Tom turn around. The ship's movement on the water was too disorienting, too unpredictable for her. She preferred to remain on land tending her garden and nurturing their daughter, Nicole.

The spring that Nicole turned three, she plucked a dandelion from the front yard. She held the delicate stem in her chubby fist and offered it up to Sharon saying, "I love you with this flower!"

Sharon had never thought of dandelions as anything more than weeds. In her daughter's hand, however, it was the most beautiful flower in the world.

It soon became a tradition, that Nicole would bring her mother the first dandelion of spring with the declaration of "I love you with this flower!" All winter long, Sharon looked forward to spring and the next love gift. When Nicole went off to college, Sharon was sure the tradition was over. But on a rainy morning in March, a card came in the mail. The card had a picture of roses on the front but inside was a smashed dandelion with "I love you with this flower!" written in Nicole's hand.

When Nicole joined the Coast Guard, Sharon got a dandelion in February from Southern California. Another year, the biggest dandelion she'd ever seen came in May from Alaska. Sharon kept all the cards and flowers in a box on the shelf next to her gardening books. After Nicole's tour was complete, she moved back into town and once again brought the dandelion in person.

Nicole joined her father on the *Jolly Roger II.*

Tom said proudly, "The sea is in her blood."

Sharon said, "I'd feel so much better if you were on land. The sea is too unpredictable, too dangerous."

To which Nicole replied, "I love the ocean, Mom. I wish I could explain it to you."

Nicole opened her laptop and showed Sharon a video of how the currents swirled from one ocean to another. Sharon watched the animated water flow in from the Atlantic, pour into the bay, and end at the rocky shore just down the hill from their house. Nicole laid out maps and charts on the kitchen table. She explained currents and depths and navigational symbols. Sharon watched her daughter run her finger along the longitudinal lines of a nautical chart as lovingly as Sharon dog-eared pages in a seed catalog. Sharon knew she had lost her daughter to the sea.

Nicole smiled. "I'm just an ocean current away, Mom."

It was a glorious autumn that year and Sharon was putting her garden to bed for the winter when the call came in from the Coast Guard. Accident. Search initiated. Husband rescued.

Then, days later, the search for Nicole was suspended. Her body went unrecovered.

A record snowfall buried the garden that winter. One day in January, Sharon walked past the bookshelf and broke down. She cried. She screamed. She pounded the floor. She pulled the box from the shelf and yanked it open. Sharon tore the cards into small ragged pieces. Tom knelt beside her, crying as well, and helped her gently place the remnants of the cards and dried dandelions back into the box.

Spring came in spite of Sharon's sorrow and she woke one morning to find a single dandelion waving to her from the front yard. It was mocking her, reminding her that she would never get another love gift from her Dandelion Girl. Sharon stomped across the lawn and yanked the dandelion up, held it in the palm of her hand about to crush the petals in her fist.

But she couldn't do it.

Instead, Sharon walked down the hill to the rocky shore. The seagulls watched as she balanced on the last rock above the waterline and thought of how her daughter was just an ocean current away. If Sharon swam far enough, dove deep enough, she would see her daughter's face again. She thought of the darkness inside of her and how the dark water matched and how it would be so peaceful and how could she possibly live without receiving a dandelion from Nicole every spring?

Sharon stood on the rocks looking at the current swirling at her feet. Then she tossed the dandelion into the dark water. "I love you with this flower," she whispered.

The dandelion bounced around on the water's surface and refused to sink.

Sharon had hoped for a sign from Nicole, that her daughter was still only a current away. Bitterly disappointed, Sharon turned to leave.

Then a motion caught her attention.

Below her, the tide turned, the current swelled and caught the dandelion up in its watery fist, offering it back to Sharon as a love gift.

Sharon heard her daughter say, "I love you with this flower!"

CHAPTER 9

AN ELOQUENCE OF CHARACTER

My bedroom window faces the mountains
and my bed faces my bedroom window
so that, on certain nights, she can wake me with
her light twinkling against the sill.

Soon, the sun will come up,
challengingly,
on the other side of the sky,
overpowering
her reflective glow with its
glaring cold brilliance.
Striding, long-legged, the sun struts with
orchestral accompaniment,
burning off fog, snubbing its nose
at the clouds.
Blazing its way forward until,
in a final triumphant bow,
it exits to the west, echoing the last chords
of its own music.

The moon rises slowly,
silently,
perhaps with the sound of a solitary
violin,
modestly gliding across the sky,
changing
her shape and mood daily,
fluidly.
Sometimes full and giving,
sometimes dark and selfish,
influencing oceans and sensitive minds.

An eloquence of character carries her through
these phases,
teaching grace and radiance and
glorious transformation.
She tugs at this woman's body
gingerly, passionately.
And I smile at her secrets and give my lover a nibble
and a nudge.

CHAPTER 10

JUST BEYOND THE SHORE

The ferry pulls into Port Sterling and I bounce in my green rubber boots. It's hard to believe that I'm really here, really doing this.

The town looks different from the water but I've been stalking it on the internet long enough to know that it hasn't changed too much in the past eight years. The ferry is the only way on or off the island unless you have your own boat or hire a seaplane. Mom loved that about Port Sterling. How quiet and pristine it was compared to other towns. And, she said, it was easy to jump off into the wilderness from here.

I heft my backpack onto my shoulder. The ferry security guard stands at the end of the ramp watching all of us disembark. The morning drizzle turns to rain, giving me a good reason to pull the hood of my blue raincoat up around my face. Even if he *is* looking for me, I'm eighteen. My ID is in my backpack. There's nothing Dad can do to stop me.

My foot hits the ground and my heart is pounding with excitement and fear. I've never been on my own before. It's a weird feeling, like being light enough to float away. I head over to the green shack on the north end of the ferry terminal, the one with the neon sign flashing B*A*I*T. I remember it from before. It's not just a bait store, it's groceries, too, even though the sign doesn't say that. Inside, I pick out a blue tarp, a pop, and beef jerky. An old guy by the magazines is reading a newspaper and complaining to another old guy behind the counter about the piss poor salmon season and seals eating his catch.

The guy with the newspaper says, "It's a damn shame we can't shoot 'em."

The guy behind the counter says, "The seals are just doing what seals do, Carl. You can't blame them for taking advantage of easy pickings."

"Sure I can. They ain't nothing but trouble."

I try not to imagine a seal with a bullet hole in her head. "The seals were here first. It's not like they can go down to the grocery store and get their food."

They turn to me like I've appeared out of nowhere.

"They can get their food someplace away from my fishing gear," Carl says.

"It's illegal to harass marine mammals."

Carl waves his hand dismissively. "Yeah, yeah, I know, I know, Marine Mammal Protection Act. Blah blah blah. If you're some kind of animal rights activist, you're wastin' your damn breath—"

The guy behind the counter interrupts, "Going hiking?"

I don't want to jinx the plan by talking about it. "Yeah."

"North?"

I nod.

Carl huffs. "Well, when you go missing, me and Stan'll tell the Troopers to just look north. Shouldn't be a problem."

Stan shakes his head. "Don't tease the girl, Carl. You were young once, too."

"At least when I was a kid, I knew better than to go hikin' alone with nothing but pop and beef jerky."

Stan adds up my purchases and I hand over my debit card.

"You know ..." He squints to read my name on the card. "... Stephanie, it's dangerous out there alone. Your family knows where you're going, right? When to expect you home?"

I mumble, "My mom taught me how to camp out here."

"Oh yeah?" Stan looks at my card again. "Trevorson? Are you Patty Trevorson's daughter? Well, sure, I see it now. You have the same brown hair and eyes and strong chin. Your mom was a friend of mine. I own a few cabins on the islands that she rented for her eco-tours. She brought you up here once, right?"

I should be happy to talk to someone who knew my mom, who remembers me, but it feels like a violation instead. Like it tarnishes my memories. All I can manage is a quick "Yeah."

Carl folds his newspaper. "I guess you don't have any more sense than your mother. She was always walking around like Mother Nature was her best friend. I'll tell you what," he says, jabbing his index finger at me, "Mother Nature's a bitch."

Carl is a dick.

Stan says, "A couple of my cabins are vacant since the season's pretty much over. Do you want to stay in one? Free of charge?"

I shove the supplies into my backpack. "I'll be fine." Then, since he'd been a friend of Mom's, I add, "Thanks anyway."

"Let me give you a map—"

"I'll be fine."

I let the door slam behind me so he knows I mean it. I don't need his cabins, his Plan B. Plan A will work. It has to.

I follow the rocky shore north until I'm the only person in the middle of nowhere. But I'm not alone. It's me and the trees and the water and the fog and the rain. Orange and purple sea stars congregate in piles on the grey rocks. I pick my way slowly so I don't step on them. One brilliant orange star is on its back, the tips of its arms curling, its tiny tube feet outstretched, a million pedicellariea grasping for something to cling to but finding only empty space. I feel sorry for it, for its futile but unrelenting ambition to orient itself properly in the world. I flip it over. It sighs and anchors itself to the rocks. One arm tip curls up in a salute.

"You're welcome."

As the day passes, the tide rises and I head for higher ground, up between the boulders into the forest. I step into a small clearing where red cedars sway, branches entwined like children's hands. One large drop of water falls from a branch and splashes on the top of my head like a blessing.

I pitch my tent among the cedars, set up the blue tarp for rainwater collection, and gather the largest rocks I can carry for a fire ring. I stack twigs over moss and strike my flint and—there!—fire and warmth and light. With survival taken care of, I allow myself to walk out to the boulders that hold back the sea. There are no boats, no planes, no signs of people. I close my eyes and take a deep breath. Then everything goes still.

I open my eyes.

She's there, just beyond the shore, watching me.

I say, "I'm back."

She disappears beneath the dark water.

Mom took me camping on my tenth birthday. She'd declared it a girls-only excursion and we left Dad behind, which she never did unless she was taking clients out. It was late in the season but I remember those five days filled with sunshine and s'mores and tide pools. On the last day—my actual birthday—my life changed forever.

Mom and I had climbed out on the rocks to catch some fish that morning. Mom showed me how to cast out the line and reel it in so it wouldn't get hung up on the boulders. Then she handed the rod over to me. "I'm going to sit over here and let you show me how it's done," she'd said.

Somewhere in the distance, a seal barked.

I was proud that Mom had faith in my skills. I leaned back and cast again. I twisted around a bit to make sure she was watching. She wasn't. She was frowning, looking out at the water. My heart and left foot slipped. I tumbled off the rocks and fell into the bay.

The frigid water was a shock. I surfaced, gasping for air. The cold clamped down on my chest. My legs and arms cramped up. The current surged. Water filled my boots and pulled me down. I kicked. I fought. I broke water again and spotted Mom scrambling down toward me, pulling her boots off as she went. My blue raincoat hood filled and dragged me down. Salt water pushed against my ears, my nose, pried my lips apart. A wave smashed me against the rocks. Then everything went still. The bubbles of my breath sparkled up to the surface; the sky wavered like a silver lid above me. I was surrounded by dark water that went on forever. And I heard it, the voice of the ocean whispering, deep-pitched and salty.

I hung there, peacefully, with only the sound of my heartbeat and the ssshusssh of the sea.

A form swam out of the darkness, grey and graceful. She floated up to me with her long dark hair floating around her. Sunlight burst through the water. She reached out her hand, seaweed wrapped around her wrist like a bracelet. She smiled, wiggled her fingers to invite me to join her. I struggled to get my feet beneath me, to kick forward, my hand stretched out to hers.

Water filled my lungs as I asked her, "What's your name?"

Meredith.

There was an explosion and my mother appeared above me.

Meredith darted away.

Mom dragged me, gagging and choking, back onto land.

I wanted to scream at her that she'd ruined everything, but all I could do was vomit up the sea and cry.

THREE DAYS AFTER MY RETURN, I'm ready. I straighten up my camp, douse the fire, and walk out onto the boulders that hold back the sea.

It's my nineteenth birthday.

She surfaces without a sound or ripple. Her whiskers twitch as she waits for me.

I kick off my rubber boots and shed my blue raincoat and jump off into the water.

The frigid water shocks me, then pushes against my ears and nostrils and lips, trying to replace the oxygen in my body. The undercurrent grabs my legs and sucks me down. Another wave catches me, smashes me against the rocks. I grapple for something solid but I'm torn away again. I break the surface, get sucked down again. I hold my breath and kick frantically. My lungs burn, my heart pounds in my ears. I try to orient myself in the world of waves and surf but find only empty water. This was not how it was supposed to be. There's no quiet, suspended-in-time feeling. There's no Meredith swimming toward me. A wave pushes me into another boulder and my held breath breaks from my lungs in a rush and I'm surfacing, gagging, clutching, dragging myself onto shore.

I push my hands into my armpits and stand, shivering.

Just beyond the shore, her brown eyes rise up and her nose twitches. She stares at me staring at her.

I want to follow her more than I've ever wanted anything.

But when the moment came, that moment I'd been dreaming of, planning for, when it finally came ... I couldn't do it. I lost my nerve.

I want to scream at her, ask her why she hadn't come for me, but all I can do is vomit up the sea and cry. I want to be back in my room where it's warm and dry and Aunt Delia is calling me down for dinner. I've made a terrible mistake, thinking I could recapture that perfect moment with Meredith. Like I could recapture that perfect trip with my mother before...the thoughts start forming in my brain, like smoke filling a balloon, and I clamp my hands over my ears and squeeze my brain so the thoughts can't take shape into words that will echo in my head. I can't let them take shape. I can't bear to hear them.

"This is kidnapping, you know," I huffed from the back seat of our Subaru.

"No it's not," Dad had said as we drove away from our house.

"What's Mom going to say when she comes back and finds us gone?"

Dad glanced at me in the rearview mirror. His face was twisted up and he looked at me with pity for a moment before looking away. "She's been lost for a month, Steph," he said in the quiet way that all the adults talked to me after my mom disappeared.

"Just because they found her kayak and not her doesn't mean anything," I argued. Thoughts started to form in my brain, like smoke filling a balloon. I squeezed my head with my hands to keep the thoughts from forming words.

"The sun actually shines in Las Vegas," Dad said. "You'll love it."

"I'll die in Las Vegas."

"You'll get used to it."

"I'm going to run away. I'm going to come back here."

"When you're eighteen years old, you can do whatever you want. But you're still a kid and I'm still your father and we're moving to Las Vegas. Aunt Delia is excited to have us live with her."

When I unpacked my clothes at Aunt Delia's house, my blue raincoat was gone. Dad had donated it to Goodwill along with all of Mom's equipment.

I never forgave him for that.

A HUGE STORM blows in before I can pack my gear and return to Port Sterling in disgrace. I'm forced to hunker down for days. I can't get the fire burning quite as well as before, can't get warm enough, can't get my clothes completely dry. I don't have any food stashed away because I thought I would be gone. Other than trying to gather burnable wood and scavenge for food, there's not much to do except stare out at the choppy water. Meredith hasn't shown her face again, and I assume she's so disappointed with me that she moved on.

When the storm passes, the beach is littered with cans of coffee and ramen noodles. A container must have fallen off a ship ... or maybe it was a blessing, a gift from Meredith. Or my mom.

I make the ramen noodles and they fill me up with warmth and my stomach stops growling for the first time in days. I don't like coffee but the plastic containers could be helpful. I'm optimistic and feeling good about my plan again. I won't fail next time Meredith shows up.

A BOAT ENGINE whines in the distance. It's Stan and Carl in an aluminum skiff with a single outboard engine. Before I can hide, Stan spots me and holds up his hand. Carl beaches the skiff and both men pull it up onto shore.

"Good to see you, Stephanie," Stan says, holding out his hand to shake. "How's it going?"

Stan's a good guy and it's hard to be mad at him, even if he did just invade my beach. I shake his hand. "I'm good."

Carl joins in. "Shit, you stink. Ain't girls supposed to be neat and tidy with makeup and nail polish?"

It's a lot easier to stay pissed at Carl. "No one's forcing you to stay."

"Take it easy, you two," Stan smiles. "She looks fine to me. You're getting enough to eat?"

I direct my answer at Carl. "There's a lot to eat out here if you know what you're looking for," I say, not mentioning that I hadn't been doing so well before the ramen noodles appeared.

Stan claps me on the shoulder with a cheerful laugh. "Just like your mom. That woman could find food when you swear there wasn't a bite to eat anywhere."

Carl holds up a grocery bag. "We brought coffee. Hope you got a fire."

"Of course I have a fire," I say and lead them up to my camp. "I have plenty of coffee, too. Lots of cans washed up on shore the other day."

"Really? We got nothing in Port Sterling."

It makes me feel good that they didn't get anything—it makes it feel more like a gift just for me.

"This is a great set-up," Stan says and sits on one of the logs near the embers I banked for the day. Carl grabs a stick, pokes the embers to life, and adds a few more twigs as if he has that right.

I snatch the stick away from him. "I'll do it. You'll mess it up."

Carl rolls his eyes. "I was doing this before you were born." He pulls a jug out of the grocery bag. "Didn't know if you had much fresh water."

I nod at the blue tarp water collection system.

Stan whistles through his teeth. "Darn good system. Did your mom teach you that?"

"Yeah."

"Looks pretty good." Carl sounds disappointed. He fills a metal teapot with water and sits it in the flames. "Guess your dad didn't have to worry about you after all."

"You talked to my dad?"

"No. The Troopers called us. He reported you missing and said you might be up here. We told them we'd come look for you."

"I'm nineteen. I don't need his permission."

Stan says, "He's worried about you. There are a lot of ways to die out here—." His words stumble, end abruptly.

"That's the truth," Carl says. "Mother Nature's a bitch. You want coffee?"

"No."

He pulls a pop out of the grocery bag. "This suit you better?"

This bit of kindness surprises me. "Thanks."

"Sure. We ain't so bad. We liked your mom, we really did." He takes off his jacket and wraps it around his hand to use like a potholder as he pulls the pot out of the fire. Stan gets a plastic funnel from the bag, fits a filter into it, as well as a few spoonfuls of coffee grounds. Carl pours the water slowly through the grounds and passes the cup to Stan before pouring his own cup. "Hard to believe she drowned. But anything can happen out here–even if you know what the hell you're doing."

I don't say anything, just stare at the flames and palm the can of pop. I remember bits and pieces of when Mom went missing. I've looked up the newspaper articles. Stan and Carl's talking eventually draws my mind to little things like the weather and what was happening out in the world. I start asking questions and before you know it, I'm thinking that it would be nice to sleep in a warm bed and watch TV. The men drain their cups and gather their stuff. Stan promises to let the Troopers know that I'm fine.

"Unless you want to come back with us. We can wait while you break camp," Stan offers. The temptation is incredible. I mean, if I can't even get my shit together enough to swim out to Meredith, if she hasn't returned, if I'm not good enough...all the thoughts, those smoke-in-the-balloon thoughts come crowding in then. I have to stop them–

Somewhere in the distance, a seal barks.

I spot Meredith just beyond the shore.

"God-damned salmon thief," Carl says and throws a rock at her. She dives. Gone. Again. Maybe forever.

"Leave her alone!"

"You comin' or not?"

"Not."

He shrugs and heads for the skiff.

"Are you sure?" Stan asks. "The weather is going to turn very soon. We might not be able to get back up here for a while."

"I'm sure," I say even though I am definitely not sure.

He shoves a piece of paper into my hand, turns, and follows Carl.

I uncrumple the paper. It's a map to his cabins.

The skiff chugs off across the bay. Stan swivels around to look for me. He raises a hand. I could stop him. I could go back.

Meredith surfaces. She watches me. Judging my worthiness.

I throw the map into the fire as the skiff disappears from view. I don't need a Plan B, Plan A will work. It has to.

SHE COMES ASHORE THAT NIGHT, in her young woman's body with her brown hair and eyes and strong chin. Her lips are soft and pink and her breasts are smooth and round. She reaches out her hand, seaweed wrapped around her wrist like a bracelet. I unzip my sleeping bag and she lays beside me and speaks in the language of the ocean, deep-pitched and salty. She tastes like secrets. We lay there with only the sound of our heartbeats and the ssshusssh of the sea.

I WAKE UP ALONE.

I stumble out of my sleeping bag, pull on my blue raincoat, and run to the water, yelling "Meredith!"

She waits for me just beyond the shore, her seal eyes and nose above the water. I walk out, picking my way carefully through a mob of sea stars. A brilliant orange star is prying a small clam open. I hesitate, torn between saving the clam or letting the sea star have its meal.

Meredith barks, reminds me what's important.

I scramble out onto the boulders that hold back the sea

before it's too late. I keep calling to her, "Don't leave me, please don't leave me!"

My heart pounds. My head aches—it's not smoke filling a balloon anymore. It's an explosion trying to shatter my skull. I clamp my hands over my ears and squeeze my brain so the thoughts can't take shape into words that will echo in my head. *How could I think I could recapture that perfect trip with my mother before ...?* I can't let them take shape. I can't bear to hear them. I lean forward, squat like I'm going to throw up. But instead of my guts, it's my heart that cracks open wide, and my head, too, and the thoughts come gushing out of me—I couldn't let myself think that Mom was dead, that she was gone forever, that I'd never see her again. But if she hadn't died, then she'd left me. The wilderness had called to her and she'd gone. She'd left her little girl. Because, somehow, I wasn't good enough.

I look up at Meredith. She looks sad. So sad. And here I am, crying like a kid.

She disappears beneath the dark water.

I wouldn't let Meredith leave me, too.

I kick off my green rubber boots and shed my blue raincoat and jump off into the sea. I gasp as the frigid water shocks me. I dive as the cold clamps down on my chest. I dive as far as I can, past the selfish surf and current. The bubbles of my breath sparkle up to the surface; the sky wavers like a silver lid above me. I'm surrounded by dark water that goes on forever. I hear it now, the sound of the ocean whispering, deep-pitched and salty. I hang there, peacefully, with only the sound of my heart-beat and the ssshusssh of the sea, waiting.

Her body drifts beneath me. She glides closer, her brown hair streaming around her body, her brown eyes shining with love. Sunlight bursts through the water around us. She reaches out her hand, seaweed tangled around her wrist like a bracelet.

She smiles and wiggles her fingers to invite me to join her. I struggle to get my feet beneath me, to kick forward, my hand stretching toward her. My breath whooshes out in a mass of bubbles as I laugh with the joy of being enough. Water fills every empty place inside of me. My vision dims around the edges. My head pounds. My heart screams.

Meredith.

Our fingers touch.

All my doubts and fears pour out of me and drift up in the sunlight with the bubbles of my last breath.

She grabs my wrist and pulls me down.

CHAPTER 11
PIGEON

Yesterday, at the library, I found a book about demonology right next to *The Sibley Guide to Birds*. Sometimes books get shelved in the wrong place and I guess that's what happened with this one. I didn't understand a bunch of the words but I looked up "demonology"—the study of demons—on the public-use computer. I knew all about Satan and his legion of fallen angels from school.

The book had scary drawings of ghosts and crazy creatures with horns and hooves and long tails, but some of the demons looked like birds. Especially the big demon with red eyes, goat feet, and beautiful, black raven wings. It looked big enough to fly me and Mom far away.

I took the book and hid behind a chair in the back of the library. It was almost six o'clock, so the library was quiet. I guess a lot of the kids were home eating dinner with their moms and talking about what they loved about their day. My mom wouldn't get home from her job across town at the Red Rooster for another hour, so I was supposed to stay at the library until seven o'clock.

From what I could figure out, the book explained how to get the demons to do things for you. The book called it "summoning" and "demanding obedience." The book said that all I had to do was draw a special diagram on the floor with chalk and say the right words, and the demon would appear and do whatever I wanted. The words I had to say were in a strange language but I thought maybe I could sound them out, like when I learned to read. Some of the people in the pictures looked gross with blood all over them. I skipped over those and I went back to the demon bird. I looked hard at that picture. The demon bird looked hard right back at me. Like it saw me.

I knew I had to take the book home with me because I'd never remember all those words or what to draw. But if the nuns caught me with something like this, they'd freak out. My school costs lots of money but I get a scholarship meant to "lift up underprivileged Catholics." Mom and I aren't Catholic but I play the part because I'm smart enough to know that I need to go to a good school and get good grades so I can go away to college. Andy, who lived three trailers away from me, went away to college and never came back. Not even for Christmas.

It was exactly seven o'clock when I used the self-checkout and stuffed the book into my backpack and ran all the way back to Mom's boyfriend, Ray's, trailer at the Boulevard Trailer Court. It's just twenty-four trailers lined up along a u-shaped road with cars and trucks parked all over the place. There aren't any trees or bushes growing anywhere. I don't know why Ray makes such a big deal about it but he reminds Mom that this is his trailer every night when they drink and scream at each other. I think the trailer is older than Mom. There are two bedrooms and one bathroom, where I wash my uniform every night as best I can in the little green sink. Mom says that Ray doesn't like kids, so I have to be invisible when he's around. It makes me mad that Mom loves Ray more than she loves me. We used to be a family even though we never sat around the dinner table and talked about our day. Then we moved in with Ray.

When I finally got to the trailer court, it was dark and there were three cop cars with their lights flashing. Red and blue bounced off all the metal houses and made the trailer court look like it was the Fourth of July. Everyone was standing around, whispering to each other. Mrs. Triscano peeked out through her curtains. I had a terrible feeling in my stomach that had nothing to do with being hungry. The cop cars were parked in front of Ray's trailer. My face felt hot and cold at the same time.

Mom yelled, "You can't arrest me! It was self-defense!"

Then Ray yelled, "I love you, babe!"

And Mom yelled back, "I'm so sorry, Ray! I didn't mean to hurt you!"

And Ray started crying, "Babe! Why you want to hurt me when I love you?"

And Mom was crying, too, "I'll be back in the morning when they let me out."

I held my breath and waited for her to tell the cops that she couldn't go to jail, that she had a daughter who needed her. I wished so hard for her to say those things. Instead, she kept saying, "Ray! Ray! Ray!"

A cop forced Mom into the back of his car and they drove away. I hid in the dark. I heard the cops asking Ray about me, where was I? He told them he didn't know; shouldn't I be in school or something? The cop said school's been out for hours. Hasn't Ray seen me today? Ray shook his head. The cherry on his cigarette glowed. He didn't know where "that brat" went during the day. The cop told Ray not to worry, they'd look for me. The cop called for CPS using the radio on his shoulder.

Child Protective Services. CPS took kids away and they

never came back. Not like Andy did – they don't fly away to college. I heard stories from the other kids. I would never see Mom again if CPS found me.

⚬

I HID in my secret spot under Ray's trailer. I'd thought about going to Mrs. Triscano's to see if I could spend the night with her. She'd probably give me macaroni and cheese and we'd watch *Wheel of Fortune* and then she'd tuck me in on her couch and Mom would be home in the morning and everything would be ok. I used to go over to Mrs. Triscano's house after school. She loves birds, too, and even makes her own bird-feeder out of an empty milk jug. It was really cool. Every morning, she stands on her front porch in her flowered bathrobe and tosses bread to the pigeons. They're just common rock pigeons, grey with black bands and shiny green and blue neck feathers. Common doesn't mean stupid, though. Those birds know that Mrs. Triscano will feed them, so they meet up on the trailer roofs and wait. They bob their heads as they walk and make cooing noises that sound like "You! You! You!" when they talk to each other. They puff themselves up and spread their tail feathers. I think they're saying that they see each other.

My name is Pigeon. Mom says I looked like a baby bird with white fuzz hair when I was born. I still have white hair that sticks out because Mom cuts it with kitchen shears. But she thought I looked like a baby pigeon when I was born, and, even though the nuns called me Donna, my real name's Pigeon.

Ray says that pigeons are flying rats and that Mrs. Triscano's crazy and someone'll get a disease someday. He says there's better things to spend money on besides bird seed. I think he means beer. One day I saw Mrs. Triscano talking with

Ray while he was fixing his truck. They started yelling at each other and then Mom told me to go to the library after school from then on.

I didn't want to make any trouble. I stayed in my hiding spot and fell asleep and dreamed that Mom and I still lived at the Sunset Motor Lodge and were eating Spaghettios and watching *Wheel of Fortune*. Then Ray busted in the door and dragged Mom away. The dream woke me up and I didn't know where I was at first. It was dark and quiet and I wasn't in my bed. Then I remembered.

I climbed out from under the trailer. The full moon was in the sky looking like it was smiling at me. Some of the pictures in the demonology book showed a full moon. So, I took the book out of my backpack and drew the circular diagram in Ray's dirt backyard with my finger. I tried to make each mark perfect even though it wasn't in chalk on a wooden floor like the pictures showed. I walked around the circle three times, saying the words as best I could. I would summon a giant demon from hell. It would be huge and breathe fire and have big wings and claws and a horrible face.

Nothing happened.

I tried again.

Nothing.

Maybe I hadn't said the words right.

I held the book carefully in the moonlight and followed the directions again; three turns around the wheel, it said, while chanting the incantation. I was pretty sure that meant to walk around the circle three times while I said the words. I did it again, being very careful with my pronunciation. I squeezed my eyelids shut and made fists with my hands. I concentrated very hard.

"You have to help me," I said out loud.

Then I opened my eyes.

A red flame started, like a red sparkler. It looked like there were two of them. It was too bright to look at so I covered my eyes with my hands. I had to look, though. I spread my fingers just a little bit to see what was happening.

All of a sudden, the red flame popped and burned out, and the air smelled like rotten eggs. I lowered my arms to see what I had summoned from the Gates of Hell.

A common rock pigeon looked at me, startled. Then it fluffed itself up and made a few cooing noises—You! You! You!—while bobbing its head stupidly. It looked at me. Its eyes glowed red.

"You gotta be kidding me," I said to the moon. "A pigeon? How's a pigeon gonna help me? He's not even big enough to fly me and Mom away."

The pigeon tilted its head this way and that, getting a good look at me. It fanned out its tail and strutted. The moonlight glittered off its neck feathers.

I felt kinda bad for insulting it; I could see it was doing its best.

"Yes, you're an excellent demon pigeon," I told it. "But I need something a little bigger, maybe with talons to hold onto us?"

The pigeon stopped strutting and stared at me for a few seconds, then it flew up into the sky. One feather fell off its tail and landed on the dirt in front of me. I picked it up—it looked like a normal feather. The tip was pointy and sharp.

I was disappointed that my experiment didn't work. I wanted to go to bed and dream about watching TV with Mom again. I didn't think that CPS would come looking for me in the middle of the night, so I piled up some pallets and climbed through the window into my bedroom.

My room is full of birds. I cut out pictures of them from the magazines in the library's free bin and tape them to my walls.

Once, I found a red ribbon on the street and tied feathers to it, then hung it in front of my window so it would blow around in the breeze.

When I'm older, I'll go to college for ornithology—that's the study of birds. Sometimes, I dream about being a bird. But even in my dreams, I'm too small to fly me and Mom away from Ray's trailer.

I laid down on my bed and twirled the demon feather between my fingers and thought of how I would try to summon a really big demon tomorrow. I scratched the word FLY into the skin of my arm with the sharp tip. The lines were white, like the chalk diagrams in the book. I did it again. And again. I did it so many times that blood welled up. I thought of the pictures in the book, of the gross bleeding people. I spelled out my own incantation with my blood. FLY.

SOMEONE KNOCKING on the front door wakes me up. Ray starts cursing and yelling about how early it is. I look at my arm and see FLY in thin scabs. I peek out and there's a woman standing in the doorway, wearing a dark blue dress suit.

She says to Ray, "I'm here to check on Donna."

Ray scratches his head, and I wonder if he even knows who Donna is.

I know this is the CPS lady. She can't find me—she'll take me away. Mom is coming home soon. I need to be here when she does. I close the bedroom door and open my window really quietly. Just before I jump out, I hear a scratching noise. The demon pigeon is looking over the edge of the broken gutter with its red eyes. It tilts its head from side to side. It says, "You! You! You!"

I stand on the window ledge and grab the gutter instead of

jumping to the ground. The metal creaks and the edges cut my fingers, but I pull myself up and over. The demon pigeon waits for me on the flat trailer roof with lots of his friends. These pigeons don't have red eyes; they're regular pigeons. They're a flock, a family. They see each other. They see me. They say "You! You! You!"

The trailer court looks really different from up here. Telephone and electrical wires hang everywhere. There's trash and lost balls and toy airplanes on the other roofs. Above me, the sky is blue and goes on forever.

The pigeons start plucking out some of their wing feathers and dropping them on the roof in front of me.

The CPS lady is calling "Donna? Donna? I'm here to help you," from the front yard.

The demon pigeon struts up to me. He bobs his head and fluffs his feathers, doing that little pigeon dance and saying "You! You! You!" I don't know why he stays here in this dirty trailer court when he could be flying in the sky and going to all kinds of cool places.

He offers me a wing feather and I take it because I don't want to be rude. "I can't go with you. I'm not a pigeon," I tell him. "And even if I were, I couldn't leave without Mom."

I hear Mrs. Triscano telling the CPS lady that she saw me sneak out my window and climb up on the roof. I thought we were friends! I thought she liked me! I'm so mad that I want to scream bad words at her and tell her that I hate her. Why can't I be invisible to Mrs. Triscano?

The pigeons are pacing around like crazy, cooing and bobbing. Mrs. Triscano is calling "Pigeon! Come on down, Honey!" and Ray is screaming "Get off my roof, you brat!" and the CPS lady keeps saying "I'm here to help you, Donna!" and Mom's voice is in my head, yelling "I'm so sorry, Ray!" I had to be invisible to Ray but, somehow, I'd gone invisible to Mom, too. I don't understand how being invisible can hurt so much, but I guess invisible doesn't mean something isn't really there. No one cares enough to see it, is all.

Even if I summoned a demon big enough to carry us both away, Mom wouldn't leave without Ray.

When she comes home, she still won't see me.

And then I'm not mad anymore. I'm ... something I don't know how to say. Something that hurts so much that I don't feel anything at all. There has to be a word for that, right?

I scratch the word FLY into my arm and whisper it. The scabs break and bleed. Flyflyfly. I push the grey feather into my skin just above my wrist. It hurts a lot. But it feels good, too. It feels like I'm a balloon stretched too tight, like I'm about to pop. The feather lets out all that extra air that's been stuck in me. I push it in real good. I don't even mind the gross blood that drips down my fingers—maybe it'll make my incantation work better.

I wipe some tears off of my face—it really does hurt—and grab another feather. I push it into my skin, higher up on my arm. It doesn't hurt as bad as the first feather. My body even feels a little lighter.

Mrs. Triscano, that traitor, tells Ray to get the ladder from her shed.

I yell, "I'm not Donna, I'm Pigeon."

I yell, "FLY! FLY! FLY!"

I push more and more feathers into my left arm, really fast, then start shoving them under the skin of my right arm. The feathers feel like they're growing from the inside out.

The top of the ladder hits the gutters with a clang.

The CPS lady says, "Come down from the roof so I can help you."

I'm not falling for that trick. I look up at the sky and I can see the wind. It moves around, like it's water but clear. It looks like a path, like a road, like something I can fly on.

The CPS lady's head pops up over the side of the roof. "Is that blood? Did Ray hurt you?"

The pigeons scatter and circle the trailer. Their wings are ragged but they have enough feathers to fly. My arms are covered in grey feathers and blood.

The demon pigeon is still on the roof. Its eyes glow red. It plucks out another wing feather and offers it to me.

The CPS lady is crawling over the edge of the roof.

There's no room left on my arms so I push the demon pigeon feather into the skin above my heart.

I squeeze my eyelids shut and make fists with my hands. I whisper "Fly!" and everything goes crazy.

The sky gets bigger and turns into blue Jell-O. But I can still breathe. I looked down at my goat feet. The demon pigeon fans out its tail and does a quick pigeon dance. It looks right at me and says, "YOU! YOU! YOU!"

Then it leaps into the blue Jell-O sky and spreads its wings. It flies like a penguin swims through water.

The CPS lady stares at me with her mouth wide open.

She sees me but she's not going to catch me.

I yell to the demon pigeon, "You! You! You!"

I jump up into the air and spread my beautiful black raven wings.

I FLY.

CHAPTER 12

DEAR COMMUNIST DOG CATCHER

Dear Communist Dog Catcher:

I'm ripping up the ticket you left taped to my front door (AC 18-0362). My little dogs are NOT neglected and my backyard is NOT full of crap and they are NOT dangerous. You just want an excuse to kill my babies. Well, this is America, not Russia, and I pay your salary with my taxes so you work for me and I'm not paying you diddly-squat.

I don't know what my ungrateful daughters told you, but I feed those dogs the best food I can afford and take them to the vet when I have the money. But my daughters wouldn't know that since they don't come around here anymore. They are too good now, with their rich husbands and their fancy houses. They look down their noses and show no respect for their mother, so what can I expect? After they moved out, child protective services stopped trying to catch me doing something wrong. But now I guess I have the Communist Dog Catcher spying on me. Don't you have some real animal abusers to arrest?

And if it wasn't my daughters who made these FALSE allegations, I bet it was the dad of that boy in Walmart last week. First off, Havoc didn't bite anyone. He's a service dog who provides me with emotional support. He has a vest that says SERVICE DOG on it, so it's official. That kid was running wild in lingerie—my baby was on a leash and minding his own business. I don't know how that kid ended up bleeding all over the place but it was not from a dog bite. I want to see the security video of the incident. Do you know that the dad and three other people ganged up on me right there in the store and said they saw Havoc grab that boy's arm? Lies! I won't let you kill my baby just because someone accused him without ANY PROOF. People like to blame pit bulls for everything but they ARE NOT VICIOUS animals. I suggest you do some research on the breed. Peanut, my Chihuahua, is really the one you should be careful of—she'll take your finger off in a minute if she gets the chance. That's why I always leave her at home. Would a bad dog owner do that? No!

Your ticket also says that my precious fur babies are not licensed. THAT IS A LIE. All four of them were licensed by my son before he left for Afghanistan. Call Camp Pendleton and check. My son took care of his responsibilities. He never gave me any grief, he sent me money every month, and he left his four dogs with me when he shipped out. It's hard to pick up all their crap every day because of my walker but I clean up as much as I can. I take good care of those babies no matter what the neighbors say.

I'm surprised your ticket didn't mention the neighbors complaining about my babies "eating the fence" as they like to call it. They're against me because my yard backs up to their big richy-rich house. It's not my fault that my dogs jump on the fence—it's their yappy little dog's fault. Havoc, Satan, and Rebel love puppies and kittens and they get overly excited when they see that Yorkie on the other side of the fence. The neighbors' allegation that my babies shove their heads through the holes in the wood fence and try to eat their dog is absolutely crazy. Pitbull heads are huge! Come out and look at it from the neighbor's side—I dare you!—since they are so concerned about their precious little Princess Bunnyfoofoo. Maybe they should replace this flimsy fence they put up with a sturdier one. They have the money.

I came home this afternoon from visiting my son's grave and found your lovely ticket. Did you wait for me to leave before you taped it to my door? Too chicken to confront a disabled old woman face-to-face? You'll never be half the man my son was. My beautiful son who died protecting my American rights. YOUR American rights, too, you ungrateful commie. I'm ripping up this ticket and I will not let you kill my son's four babies. I will take good care of them just like he took good care of me.

You can go to hell.

CHAPTER 13
MEMORIES OF THE FUTURE

The woman shifted in the white plastic chair in Exam Room #2, and picked at the hem of her purple shirt. Purple meant Tuesday. Her wife's hand touched the skin of her arm. She knew that face, that scent, that soul. But she couldn't remember that name.

A young woman entered the room. "Good morning, Lucy. How are you today?"

The word "Lucy" sent a cascade of images dropping into her mind. Lucy. That was her. Her wife's name was Gail. The other woman was a doctor. A shiver of anxiety passed through her as the word "Alzheimer's" surfaced.

"She's doing okay today," Gail said. She sounded confident, so Lucy tried not to worry that she couldn't find the words to answer the doctor. As long as Gail was there, she was safe.

Gail and the doctor talked, then Gail squeezed her arm and said, "The experimental drug sounds promising. Do you want to be in the test trial?"

The word "experimental" confused her, but Gail's tone was hopeful.

Lucy nodded her head.

AT FIRST, the memories came in clumps and flashes. She was an old man hunched over. She crouched near a campfire in a dark jungle. She bent her back against a rough rope and hauled boulders in the blistering heat.

There were memories of Gail, too. Gail chasing chickens in a dirt yard. Gail carrying a birthday cake. Gail riding up on a black horse. Gail didn't always look the same but Lucy'd recognize her soul anywhere.

One recollection looped through her brain the most—her and Gail standing on the deck of a wooden ship. Side by side, they stared as a snowy landscape drifted past. Lucy wore a brown coat with stiff white ruffles and Gail wore a long blue dress. She held her arm out to Gail and Gail placed her hand in the crook of Lucy's elbow. Gail smiled up at her, a smile that held lifetimes of hope and love.

LUCY SHIFTED in the white plastic chair. She wore a red sweater. What day was red? Gail was talking to a young woman—Lucy dug deep and found "Alzheimer's" lurking in the dark. She wanted to run. Gail placed her hand on Lucy's arm and said, "The doctors are encouraged by your progress. I think you should keep taking this medication. Don't you?"

Gail smiled down at her with so much hope and love that Lucy couldn't disappoint her even though she didn't understand the word "medication."

She nodded her head.

THE MEMORIES SHIFTED. Flashed. Snapped. Lasted moments. Lasted lifetimes.

She was a small child in a man's arms. She swam in a pool at the top of a glass building. She stood on a rocky shore with ash falling around her.

Her new favorite memory was of her and Gail standing in the belly of a spaceship. Side by side, they stared out the port-hole as stars drifted past. Lucy wore some kind of brown outfit with white gloves and Gail was in blue. Lucy held her arm out to Gail and Gail placed her hand in the crook of Lucy's elbow. She smiled up at her, a smile that held lifetimes of hope and love.

LUCY SAT in the kitchen with a half-eaten pancake on her plate. She wore an orange cardigan. Friday. There was a crossword puzzle in front of her, the blanks filled out with random letters, as if she couldn't think of words to fill the spaces. That was bizarre—she was an astrophysicist. Of course, she could solve a simple crossword puzzle. Gail entered the room wearing a blue coat.

Lucy said, "Looks like it's gonna be a beautiful day, Gail."

Gail stared at her for a moment, then laughed. "You remember my name."

"Of course I remember your name. You're my wife. I'd know your soul anywhere."

They walked along the waterfront. They shared ice cream. They crossed Barnes Road as a green delivery truck barreled around the corner against the light. Lucy threw Gail to the sidewalk just before the bumper made contact.

Why hadn't this been one of her memories so she could avoid it?

She didn't want to leave. Not yet.

Looking down at Gail kneeling beside her body, Lucy understood. Somewhere, Gail would smile up at her with another lifetime of hope and love again.

Lucy turned away and greeted that next memory.

CHAPTER 14
I'VE LEARNED TO GIVE THEM WHAT THEY WANT

I've learned to give them what they want.
They think they're getting flamboyantmetransparent.
How were they to know I just slipped through their fingers?
Stun 'em, shock 'em, give them a brutal little tidbit of who they
think is me
and they won't see,
really,
magicalmeradiant.

CHAPTER 15

DHARMA BUMS AT STARBUCKS

Standing on the sidewalk just outside of Starbucks
is a young guy, younger than my kids, maybe mid-20s.
He's got a cell phone to his ear,
and a red suitcase at his feet
with a pristine copy of *Dharma Bums* sitting on top of it.
I'm surprised.

Most of the wannabes drag duffle bags and display ragged
copies of *On The Road* and sit in Pioneer Square demanding
money as if it were their right, as if it were payment for
reminding us all of our inauthenticity.

This kid doesn't fit the mold.

I go in and wait in line until it's finally my turn
and order my usual mocha.
The kid comes in behind me, avoids the line,
and takes a table in the corner.

He pulls an exquisite laptop from his suitcase and opens up his
email.
I'm surprised and take a closer look.

He doesn't smell of pot or patchouli or body odor and his beard
is neatly trimmed. He doesn't scan us with an air of disdain for
our selling out to corporate coffee and his clothes have high-
end logos stitched on the outside. His aura is earnest.

I want to ask him:
Where do you think you're going?
What kind of enlightenment do you think you'll find?
But I don't because I'll sound jealous and petty.
That's how I feel about this kid who doesn't fit the mold,
half my age, with money, heading out purposefully.

I collect my mocha and walk to my Subaru,
use the keyfob to beep the locks open and,
when I reach for the handle, I hear a clucking,
a tsk-tsking, the rattle of shaking heads.
I turn 360 and, from this parking lot I see:
Mount Rainier, the Cascade Range, the Olympic Mountains.

They tsk-tsk me and remind me that time is an illusion, resent-
ment is bad karma,
and the ripples of revolution move outward forever, washing
up on all shores, including mine, now.

Get moving.

CHAPTER 16

THE PAINTED PONIES OF WILEY CREEK

Every now and again, the men of Carbondale, when they got themselves all riled up and drunk, would declare that they was goin' out and getting' themselves a Painted Pony. They'd clamber up on their horses and shoot up the moon, and thunder off into the desert, nearly falling out of their saddles. In the morning they'd come crawling back with headaches and stories 'bout seeing the sparks of silver hooves in the dark, and swearin' they'd heard laughter and piano music echoing through the canyons. Once, Three-Toed Joe woke up in the middle of town with a hoof print on his forehead and no memories of the past three days as proof of such things.

On those mornings, Madam Pearl Wiley would stand on the balcony of her fine establishment on Main Street, on the opposite end of town from the First Church of Christ the Cowboy, and watch the men crawl off to their beds. She'd shake her head, then shake out the sheets, clean out the secrets and lies, and give her gals the afternoon off. She'd harness her fine bay filly to her fine black carriage and drive on out to her place—a five hundred acre spread that many a man had offered to marry her for. Pearl Wiley had no use for men, in general, discovering long ago that taking her own needs in hand was far cheaper than taking another husband. Her first and only husband, God rest his soul, had had the good sense to die quickly in a duel over something stupid. She, being the sole inheritor, had liquefied his assets and headed off toward the setting sun.

~

"Can you smell it, Bunny?" The words tore out of Clara's throat like a cactus paddle. "Can you smell the water?"

Clara dug her elbow into the sandstone dust and wrenched around to find Bunny. But her little grey mare wasn't there. She hadn't been for three days now. Clara kept forgetting that.

They were supposed to be going to California together. To be a gentleman rancher and his retired cowpony. There wasn't much point in crawling any further without Bunny. But the desire to survive wasn't letting go of Clara so easily. She hauled herself up the bluff with fingernails bleeding and skin scraping dirt and rock. Her clothes had shredded some time during the past two days but, luckily, the thick cotton bandages that bound her breasts were fairly intact. Clara figured it was only fitting that the fabric that hid her unfortunate sex would also provide some protection.

The sun was dropping toward late afternoon. Soon night would bring some relief from the heat. But then the cold would come descending like a mountain lion. Clara groaned deep in her heart and pulled herself up to the edge of the bluff.

What she saw surely could not exist.

Perhaps she was delirious with thirst.

Before her lay a long valley, appearing out of nowhere in

the south and disappearing into buttes in the north. It was narrow, only an hour's ride across on a good pony. But it wasn't the valley itself that seemed unreal. Clara'd ridden through plenty of them in her ten years moving cattle. This valley had a stripe of green grass running down its middle, like the line down a burro's back. There were even a few cottonwoods standing in a crooked line.

"There's a creek down there," she told Bunny. She said "creek" like her mama had taught her, back when she was little Clarabelle Cariveau, living in Boston. Not "crick" like she'd come to say as Clark Smith. Mama'd be proud. Maybe. Her mother was a dream, a wish. Bunny, poor Bunny with buzzards tearing out her insides because Clara had thought they could outrun a damn sandstorm, was more real to her than her mother. She ran her arm across her forehead, swiping at sweat, flies, and memories.

There was a nicker. Then a whinny. Then the mighty thunder of hooves shook the ground. Clara turned quick as her poor body could manage as the ponies came on her. No blacks or browns or greys among them—in skins of cobalt, orange, chartreuse, emerald, yellow, they pirouetted between rattlesnakes and gopher holes on gold and silver hooves. Their manes and tails flew like standards declaring freedom. They were as beautiful and tough as desert flowers and led by a stocky scarlet mare with bells jingling in her mane. And they were all running straight at Clara.

Startled that her death would come so quickly after so much suffering, Clara rolled to her stomach, covered her head with her arms, and counted down how much longer she had … three … two … one …

But instead of trampling her, the lead mare dodged right at the last minute and the river of ponies flowed around her, leaping over the edge of the butte. After the last pony passed her by, she looked down into the valley where the ponies danced in the green grass.

Their story was told around every campfire from Alberta to Abilene. The details changed some, depending on the teller, but one fact remained unchanged—the Painted Ponies danced along Wiley Creek.

The lead mare broke away from the herd and stared up at Clara. Clara's fingers twitched with the urge to grab a rope and lasso the mare, to climb onto her back and ride all the way to California. Or at least let the mare drag her to the creek hidden somewhere in the grass. The mare scratched at the ground with a silver hoof. She lowered her head and snorted. Clara heard the challenge as if the mare had spoken to her—Catch me if you can!

"You're a sly one," Clara croaked. "Even if I did have my rope, you know I don't have the strength to catch you."

The lead mare tossed her head. Yes, she surely knew.

Clara screamed, low and loud, as she hauled herself up and over, slid down, and tumbled to the valley floor. She crawled until her fingers sank into damp ground and her belly was stained green, until her short brown hair was slick with water. She sucked Wiley Creek down her throat.

The cold settled in and Clara's teeth began to chatter.

Maybe the night would accomplish what the blazing day could not.

"Oh, fuck me," Clara said as that last bit of struggling to survive whispered away. They were coarse last words, to be sure, but they seemed appropriate.

There was a rustle in the grasses. Too small to be a pony. A coyote or wolf then. Life was full of surprises.

Then a woman's voice drawled, "What do you have, Poppy?"

A face appeared above Clara: silver hair, crystal blue eyes, skin impossibly white in this desert—maybe it had been darker once and the sun had bleached it like Bunny's bones. She couldn't figure the woman's age. Old enough to be her sister? Mother? Grandmother?

The mare snorted. The woman looked Clara in the eye, looked clear down into her soul. "I guess I better get you back to the house."

CLARA STOOD in the yellowing grass of Wiley Creek. It had become her custom to watch for the painted ponies each evening, between supper and driving Pearl into town. She never witnessed their dancing and cavorting again, however.

Pearl called out from the barn, "It's getting late."

Clara turned away from the promise of ponies. She was disappointed and told Pearl so.

"They show up when they're needed," was Pearl's answer. Clara didn't know what that meant as the ponies seemed to serve no true purpose but asking Pearl questions was useless. Pearl was an odd one and didn't have a lot to say about anything.

Clara led Lulu, Pearl's brown filly, out of the barn already hitched up to Pearl's smart black rig. Pearl stepped aboard. Clara took up the reins. Lulu, with a jaunty little high step, brought them into Carbondale, to Pearl's business enterprise, the Carbondale Grand Lodge and Saloon. Pearl took in desperate women and made money off of them. Clara didn't understand how Pearl could render assistance in the form of shelter, food, and wages, and yet profit from their whoring. But asking questions on this matter proved useless as well.

At midnight, Clara handed over the stable duties to Dimwit Jericho Stutts, the only male in Pearl's employ. She went round to the back entrance, through the kitchen where Cookie always had a little something set aside for her, and headed into the saloon to buy herself a whiskey.

Gloria was at the piano, playing something rousing to promote drinking, gambling, and whoring. The saloon was full of cigar smoke, the smell of liquor, and men. Minnie appeared at the top of the stairs, adjusting her skirt. The wood creaked and complained as she eased her two-hundred-plus pounds down to the main room. A bold, purple eye-patch covered her right eye and, as she descended, Minnie lifted the patch slightly and winked at Clara with her good right eye. "You gonna buy me a drink, *Clark Smith*?"

Clara saluted with her whiskey.

One of the miners playing poker leapt out of his seat, shoutin' that the fuckin' Eye-talian across the table was a damn cheat. The piano notes spun off-kilter as Gloria ducked under her instrument. The suspected cheater pulled a gun and took a wild shot. There was a moment of thundering silence, then the crash of Minnie tumbling down the stairs, a trail of red in her wake.

All hell broke loose then, with the men fighting and blaming. Clara crawled toward Minnie while shots whizzed overhead. Then silence again as Pearl waded into the middle of the mayhem, shut down the place, and assured Sheriff Buckholzer that everything was fine, just fine, and she'd take care of everything. Sheriff Buckholzer hauled off the miners, probably to sleep it off in the jail and be released to go back to work in the morning.

Gloria returned to her piano, her fingers shaking. She closed the key cover.

"Get Lulu hitched up," Pearl told Clara. "I'm taking Minnie to the ranch."

"What the hell for? She's dead," Clara spat. Minnie's head

was cradled in her lap. Minnie had a little boy somewhere back East, a fine son who lived in a cottage by the sea. That's what Minnie had claimed, anyway. Who was going to tell him his mama'd been shot over a damn card game? "You're not going to do anything about this? You know those miners won't spend one day in prison for killing her. Nobody gives a damn about a whore, ain't that right? Not even you?"

"Get the rig," was all Pearl said over her shoulder as she climbed the stairs.

Clara stomped and cussed her way back to the stables. Sure, her wages came from the whores, too. She was a damn hypocrite talking about the money they brought in and then taking it herself. But it just wasn't right how Pearl was handling Minnie's death. With a heavy heart and conflicted mind, Clara harnessed Lulu up and drove the rig around to the back door of the saloon. Cookie opened the door and Pearl hauled out a rolled-up carpet. It was surely too heavy for Pearl but there she was, hefting the bloated carpet into the back of the rig like Clara flung bales of hay over her shoulder.

Pearl stepped up next to Clara and looked clear down into her soul.

And Clara realized, like being kicked by a longhorn in the gut, that she wanted Pearl to see clear on down to Clarabelle.

They rode home in silence.

At the ranch, Pearl hefted the bundle and started walking. Clara followed across the dirt yard, past the barn and garden, past the farmyard, down through yellowing grass and wet of Wiley Creek. They walked past one, two, three cottonwoods stripped of leaves. Pearl nodded for Clara to stay put. She walked a bit further, then laid Minnie down and unrolled her carpet shroud. Tears gathered in Clara's eyes. Minnie used to tease her, "How about a free ride, *Clark?*" Clara would always laugh and toss back a whiskey because neither men nor women had ever much appealed to her and Minnie hadn't cared about that one bit.

The sound of bells came gently from the East, just a sense of jingling at first, just a suggestion, then more and louder until there was no mistaking them. Clara turned and there they were—the Painted Ponies running, jumping, dancing across the desert, through the sage and bitterbrush. They came as if bidden by Pearl. But that thinking was wrong. It wasn't Pearl who drew them.

The lead mare approached with don't-mess-with-me steps, always wary, always suspicious, always protecting. She sniffed the fabric smudged with blood and the stained lace that lifted like worn daisy petals in the breeze. The scent of roses and carbolic acid rose up. The mare's teeth chomped. Her ears flicked. She stomped her foot and the bells jangled.

The fabric jerked.

A low nicker—a foal's call—then a hoof, golden and sharp, kicked out from under the dirty petticoat. The herd paced. There was a scrambling, then another foal-call to the lead mare, who offered up a mare-call. The fabric fell away as a plum-colored filly with a white spot around her right eye shook off fabric and lace, left boots behind, and struggled on her new thin legs. The filly staggered, tripped, kicked up her heels, twirled and rolled in the muck of the creek. The other ponies nuzzled and nosed her, committing her scent to memory. Then the lead mare guided the Painted Ponies back up the arroyo, never looking back at Pearl or Clara or the blood and stench of the brothels.

"CLARK?" The male voice was hoarse from trail dust and saloon smoke. "I'll be damned. It is you."

Clara pulled her persona tight as a corset and turned to face the old man in the livery doorway. She tried to remember how men talked to each other. The words. The tone. She had to dig deep to remember. "How the hell are ya, Franklin?"

"Good. Good."

Franklin's mule, Matilda, stood behind him staring blankly out to some unknown horizon. She did that sometimes. Clark always wondered what she was looking at but never did figure it out. Bunny had loved Matilda and the feeling had seemed mutual. Whenever Franklin joined them on the trail—Matilda hauling the supply wagon—Bunny preferred to be with the mule at the end of the day than with the other horses. They'd murmur to each other in the dark and sleep side by side.

For a moment, Clark felt the presence of the little grey mare. But she was gone, he reminded himself. The thought of seeing the blank space where Bunny shoulda been kept him from looking back. It still hurt. If only he hadn't …

Franklin stroked his yellowing beard. "Heard you was goin' west to California to breed horses or some such nonsense."

"That's the plan."

"Not surprised. Sure, you always did have a way with the ponies. Looks like you didn't get far."

"Winter came on me."

Franklin nodded and spit on the ground between them. It left a nasty blotch in the dirt. "Plenty warm enough now. Me and Matilda are going to Frisco. Got a cousin lives out there. He needs strong men to work the docks. We should travel together. Where's your pony? Rabbit was it?"

"Bunny."

"Yeah, that's right. What grown man calls his pony Bunny?" He spit again.

"She died."

"Ah, well, I'm sorry 'bout that." He removed his hat for a

moment. There was a second of silence. The loss of a good trail horse, one that had served well, was always respected by the men even after they drove their horses to that death. It was strange. Franklin replaced his hat and handed over Matilda's reins. "If you're comin', be ready in the morning. Be good to have an extra set of eyes looking out for danger. But for now," Franklin made a show of winking. "A hot bath and a whore'll fix me up right before that last push to the Pacific."

"I'll think on it."

Franklin walked off to the saloon, leaving Clark with Matilda and a decision to make.

Franklin was right, traveling together would be safer. But the thought of going west ... it just didn't set as well as it had under last summer's sun. As he led Matilda to an empty stall, the old mule laid her jaw over his shoulder and blew out a breath. Bunny'd always done the same. Then Matilda stumbled, caught herself, and plodded forward, never losing that blank stare. The poor mule would never see Frisco. She deserved to die in a thick bed of hay, not on the trail where she'd end up no better than Bunny. Clark's mind turned the thoughts over. Franklin was shrewd when it came to taking advantage of a situation. He'd hold out until Clark offered enough to buy a sturdy trail horse to replace the old mule. Clark had a little money stashed away. Whore money. To buy the freedom of an old mule. He wondered what Minnie would think of it. And if he left in the morning with Franklin, he'd need a horse of his own. He added up the money he'd saved. It might work. Then he'd leave Matilda with Pearl. Surely she had enough room for one more. And head West to that dream he'd had since he was Clarabelle, following her daddy around the stables.

At midnight, Clark handed over the stable duties to Jericho and headed into the saloon for a word with Pearl. But when

Clark got to Pearl's office on the second floor, she was face down at her desk, columns of numbers crawling like ants beneath her cheek. At first, Clark thought she was asleep. One touch to her cheek proved Clark wrong.

AT THE RANCH, Clara hefted the rolled up carpet that contained Pearl Wiley up onto her shoulder and walked across the dirt yard, past the barn and garden, through the new green grass and wet of Wiley Creek. She walked past one, two, three cottonwoods with hopeful budding leaves. She walked a bit further and laid Pearl down.

The sound of bells came gently from the East, just a sense of jingling at first, just a suggestion, then more and louder until there was no mistaking them. There was the unfurling of the carpet, the nickering and whinnying, the rustle of fabric. A silver filly, pale as the moon danced as lithe and strong as a prima ballerina. Then all the Painted Ponies looked clear on down into her soul.

And Clara realized that they could see clear on down to Clarabelle Cariveau.

"I guess I'll be staying here."

The lead mare snorted and tossed her head, then spun and led them all back up the arroyo, never looking back, the new silver filly glowing like moonlight.

As Clara turned to leave, a flash of white caught her attention. She leaned over the slow water of Wiley Creek. Pearl's face gazed back at her, silver hair and clear eyes and skin as white as bones bleached by the sun. Bunny laid her jaw across Clara's shoulder and blew out a breath.

"Ain't life full of surprises?" Clara asked her little grey pony. "It's kind of like raising up horses. Don't you think?"

EVERY NOW AND AGAIN, the teenaged boys of Carbondale, when they got themselves all riled up and drunk, would declare that they was goin' out and gettin' themselves a Painted Pony. They'd clamber into jacked-up pickups and crank up the radio, and thunder off into the desert, nearly falling out of the truck beds. In the morning they'd come crawling back with headaches and stories about seeing the sparks of silver hooves in the dark, and swearin' they'd heard laughter and piano music echoing through the canyons. Once, Chad Bradley woke up in the middle of the football field with a hoof print on his forehead and no memories of the past three days as proof of such things.

On those mornings, Ms. Pearl Wiley would emerge from the office of her fine establishment on Main Street, on the opposite end of town from the First Church of Christ Our Savior, and grab a latte at the Starbucks on the corner. She'd shake her head, then shake the hand of her financial advisor, review the income and expenses, and hire more staff at a livable wage. She'd fire up her candy apple red 1969 Corvette and drive on out to her place—a five hundred acre spread that many a man had offered to buy for oil drilling or data storage. Pearl Wiley had no use for the money they threw at her, discovering long ago that women would always come to the Carbondale Lodge & Spa looking for a new life. She, being the sole proprietor, kept her properties intact and, when the time was right, watched for the Painted Ponies of Wiley Creek.

About the Author

Elizabeth Beechwood is your typical scarf-knitting, bird-feeding tree hugger who lives on the western fringes of Portland, Oregon. When she writes, she starts with regular people with regular lives … but then something strange happens. Whether it's fiction, fantasy, magical realism or genre-bending, you can count on something just a little peculiar from her stories.

She earned an MFA in Popular Fiction at the University of Southern Maine's Stonecoast program and is a member of SFWA and Willamette Writers.

When she's not writing, she loves facilitating writing workshops, walking through wild places, and spoiling her cats.

www.ingramcontent.com/pod-product-compliance
Lightning Source LLC
Chambersburg PA
CBHW031546310726
48971CB00008B/2648